The Adventures of Daring Dog

Charlotte Jerace

SOAR

Charlotte Jerace

ISBN: 1496098110
ISBN 13: 9781496098115
Library of Congress Control Number: 2014904072
CreateSpace Independent Publishing Platform
North Charleston, South Carolina

To Minna Hart and Kaia Ellie

A strong imagination is a gift you both possess.
Use it to bring joy to the world

For Penny and Stella

In Memory of Pedro, Zsa Zsa, Clover, Worm, Sam and Gogo
Devoted friends

He is your friend, your partner, your defender, your dog. You are his life, his love, his leader. He will be yours, faithful and true, to the last beat of his heart. You owe it to him to be worthy of such devotion. – Unknown

TEXTING TRANSLATION – I used as my reference http://transl8it.com/.

TEXT	ENGLISH
Yor K9 iz ugLE	Your dog is ugly
sO R U!	So are you
Yor ugLE 2!	You're ugly too
Yor a jerk	You're a jerk
BetA kEp yor eye on d K9	Better keep your eye on the dog
wntd	Wanted
cNtR	Center
h/w	Homework
jst	Just
K	Okay
Txt	Text
Bff	Best friends forever
Wat	What
nEd 2 practiS	Need to practice
L8r	Later
Kewl	Cool
werd n d car	Weird in the car
truk	Truck
wot wz	What was
w8N 4 d grEn lite	Waiting for the green light
Y	Yes
U shud hav cn her	You should have seen her
TLK	Talk
wz it rly	Was it really
NothA	Another
jst had 2 b pAtNt	Just had to be patient
Onr	Owner
Myn	Mine
U R a 3: o)	You are a girl

Introduction

~

MISTY HARBOR LIGHTHOUSE KEEPER'S COTTAGE
1 a.m.

Blue. Not the color of the sky or the ocean, but a blue like I have never seen before. It's cold, I'm freezing and I can't see my mom. Who's calling my name? Don't move, Sam, we can see you – you're going to be fine. We're coming to get you ... You're okay, Sam. Promise.

"**M**om!" Sam screamed.

"Sam, wake up! You're having a bad dream," Davidson Harris said while tapping the shoulder of his ten-year-old son who was writhing in his bed in the grips of a vivid nightmare. His blankets and pillows were in a crumpled heap on the floor. When he felt his father's touch, Samuel Harris awakened suddenly. For a moment, he forgot where he was.

"It's so real, Dad, it's like I'm there again," Sam said, while rubbing his eyes and pulling himself up on his pillows. He was covered with sweat, and yet he was shivering.

Mr. Harris felt a twinge in his chest as he took his son's trembling hand. "Talk to me, Sam, tell me about this dream you keep having and we can try to make it go away."

His father tried to put his arms around Sam, but like many boys his age, Sam pulled away.

"I can't," Sam whimpered, wiping his tears on the edge of his quilt.

"Try, Sam, get it off your chest," his dad urged softly.

Sam remained silent, his eyes focused on the quilt's pattern. He was tired of seeing his father's concern every time he'd had a nightmare.

Mr. Harris waved his right hand over Sam's chest. In a split second his WELLBEENER twirped **"PULSE 120, TIME: 1:19 A.M."**

Sam's pulse was racing faster than it had during his last nightmare.

"Take a deep breath," Mr. Harris said calmly. Reluctantly, Sam opened his mouth, took a gulp of air, and then squeezed his eyes shut. After a few seconds he shook his head, blinked hard and released his breath.

"Better?" his dad asked, as he reset the WELLBEENER – a device he had invented. The paper-thin wrist band could measure a patient's pulse and blood pressure with just a wave of his hand – no blood pressure cuff, nothing. It was just the magic of technology.

"Yeah, I guess so," Sam grunted.

"I know you don't like to hear this, but it will make you feel better if you talk about it, I promise," his dad said. He knew that the longer Sam stayed quiet about the accident, the more he would suffer.

"Don't ever say 'promise' to me, Dad," Sam answered sharply. His lower lip quivered as he slid deep beneath the covers.

Mr. Harris dropped his chin, and then his stooped and bony shoulders sagged. He wasn't sure which was worse – Sam's physical injuries or the emotional pain that his son refused to speak about.

"Lean forward while I fluff up your pillows, Sam."

The boy didn't budge. "Sorry I woke you, Dad."

His father shook his head. "No son, don't ever be sorry that you need me. He waved his WELLBEENER over Sam's chest, relieved to see that his heartbeat had slowed back to normal. "Is there anything I can get for you, maybe some hot chocolate, or a glass of milk?"

"No," Sam said flatly. "You *know* you can't get me what I want."

1

Royal Scent Kennels, Forrestdale, Maine

~

Mrs. Prudie Mason drove her van down the long bumpy road that cut through the thick Maine forest leading to her home. Although winter had barely begun, she was already tired of the bone-chilling, cold weather. Even so, she had to admit that it was a spectacularly beautiful day. The November sun hung low in the bright blue sky, casting a shimmering light on the snowy branches of the towering pines that lined the road to her home. *It's not even Thanksgiving and we've already had a big snowstorm*, she realized.

Next to her, a scrappy little nine-week-old puppy was trying to munch on Mrs. Mason's down-filled coat. She'd brought this puppy along so she could observe her more closely. The pup had been sneezing non-stop, almost since birth.

"Leave it," she said firmly, giving the command that the puppy's brothers and sisters had already learned to obey. But this puppy ignored her, tugging harder while sinking her tiny, sharp teeth into the sleeve of Mrs. Mason's favorite winter coat. A stray down feather escaped the pinpricked hole that the puppy's teeth had opened.

"Leave it!" Mrs. Mason commanded, louder and sharper this time. The puppy ignored her again and held her ground, pulling and tearing at the coat until they arrived home.

A plume of smoke curled from the chimney of the Masons' rambling, picture-perfect farmhouse. "It looks like Mr. Mason has stoked up the woodstove," Prudie Mason said to the puppy as she tried to snatch her leather pocketbook from it's little jaws.

"LEAVE IT!" Mrs. Mason shouted in frustration. Startled, the puppy looked up for a moment, then returned to her munching.

"We'll just have to work harder with you," Prudie groaned, prying her pocketbook from the little dog's mouth. "Off to your pen, with you."

Inside the house, Doug Mason was busy loading seasoned oak into their wood stove. The house was warm and comfortable, filled with overstuffed chairs and couches whose stuffing had spilled out thanks to the many dogs that had passed through the home.

After helping his wife take off her coat, Doug Mason greeted her by playfully licking her cheek and panting. Prudie matter-of-factly returned his greeting in the very same way.

"Any luck with her?" he asked hopefully.

"Not really," Mrs. Mason mumbled as she put the kettle on for tea. Then she chose a chair closest to the woodstove so she could warm her bones.

"Still sneezing?" he asked, knitting his eyebrows together.

"Yes, maybe there's something stuck up there ..." Prudie had considered this since puppies often put their noses where they shouldn't. "Maybe a pebble or a piece of kibble is lodged in her nose," she reasoned.

"Her nose looked clear to the vet," he reminded her.

"I know, I'm just hopeful, as always," Mrs. Mason answered, offering a warm smile.

Mr. Mason prepared a cup of tea in his wife's favorite bone china teacup. He set it down on the side table next to her chair. "Give me your paw," he chuckled, and then he slipped a ginger snap cookie into her outstretched hand.

"Oh Doug, you are so kind."

"You picked a winner when you chose me, Prudie!"

"Don't I know it," she answered, "a real champion, that's what you are, Doug Mason."

Her husband of forty years scratched behind his ears, rubbed his hands together, and then reached for his coat. He had many chores to do before the day ended.

"She better get with the program fast," he said as he stepped into his boots.

"You don't need to tell me, dear. I'm well aware that she might be a problem," Mrs. Mason assured him.

"Two weeks before we get on the road," he reminded her.

Mrs. Mason nodded her head from side to side, her thick lips shifting back and forth, uncannily like her bloodhounds.

Mr. Mason shivered, his teeth chattering loudly, when he stepped out into the cold. He quickly crossed the yard and entered the big red barn where he and his wife ran their business of breeding world-class bloodhounds. With their hard work and careful attention to their dogs, Royal Scent Kennels had earned the reputation as breeders of some of the world's smartest bloodhounds — dogs who can pick up a scent and track it for miles.

"A good bloodhound's nose will guide them over cliffs or into trees, their focus is so strong on finding the source of the scent they're given," Mr. Mason would explain every chance he got. "Put a shirt, or even a hairbrush under their nose and you'd better hang on to the leash. They won't stop until they can hunt it down!" Mr. Mason loved to boast about his bloodhounds. And once he got started ...

"But, those are the *good* bloodhounds." His voice would grow louder and up a pitch or two. "The dogs we breed at Royal Scent Kennels are *exceptional* bloodhounds, which is why police K-9 units from all over the country line up to buy our puppies." Then he would imitate his dogs with a loud heek, three twitches to his nose, followed by several seconds of panting.

The following day, as the Masons enjoyed a tomato soup and peanut butter sandwich lunch, they received a phone call from a Mrs. Pennyworth of Hypoluxo, Florida who'd seen a bloodhound in a movie and wanted one for a pet.

"He'll have his own room! We're on the fifth floor so there's a great view, and we have a café by the pool where I can get him whatever he wants," she gushed. "Just crate up a little male and ship him on down here to Palm Beach International Airport."

Mr. Mason couldn't help but laugh. "Sorry, ma'am, but a condo is a silly place for a dog who needs lots of exercise and a large yard to romp around in."

"I don't think you understand," she argued, "I am in *love* with bloodhounds. We'll be able to sit on my patio and watch the boats go by. What a life for him!"

Mr. Mason covered the phone so she wouldn't hear him tell Prudie, "This one's putting up a fight!"

"AHEM!" Mr. Mason cleared his throat, softened his tone.

"They're champion slobber slingers, you know," he said, using a turnoff that usually did the trick. He waited for a response but only heard Mrs. Pennyworth breathing. "Seriously, they'll decorate your walls, furniture, pictures and clothes, to say nothing of your face, with their slimy slobber in no time."

Silence for a second, then, "What's a little drool between friends?" Mrs. Pennyworth said, followed by a nervous giggle. Mr. Mason scratched behind his free ear. He thought for a moment.

"You might want to know that their tails are exactly at coffee table height and they can clear it off with one sweep!" Mr. Mason barked, cutting through the air with his arm outstretched, as if she could see through the phone. Losing his patience, Mr. Mason began to pant and pace back and forth, as Mrs. Pennyworth insisted she could handle a bloodhound.

Mr. Mason's nose began to twitch. "They eat *enormous* amounts of food. You could spend your last nickel on vet bills."

"Oh," she said quietly, "I didn't think about that. I live on a fixed income."

"Indeed," Mr. Mason sighed.

"Maybe buying a bloodhound isn't such a good idea," she relented.

"Try a Chihuahua," Mr. Mason suggested, "and make it a rescue dog, you'll be happier!"

"Well, thank you for being honest," Mrs. Pennyworth said, "that shows good character."

"Thank you, Ma'am. Just take your time before choosing a dog and make sure it is the best choice for you and for the dog. It's a big commitment."

"Good job!" Prudie beamed at her husband, and then playfully tugged his earlobe.

Mr. Mason was relieved. The last thing he needed was for someone to buy one of his puppies, only to learn later that they'd chosen the wrong pet for their lifestyle. They'd want to return it, get a refund – and if that weren't bad enough, the Masons would have to unlearn all of the pup's bad habits it had picked up in an unwelcome household.

Mind you, it isn't that bloodhounds don't make excellent pets. On the contrary, they become very attached to people and are great watchdogs. That's the good news. The bad news is that the sound of their baying has been described as the sound of a moose in pain.

"Ow-wow-wow-argh-argh-ooo-ooo," – or something like that.

That could be troublesome for someone without a lot of room and a good distance from their neighbors. However, with their large barn, huge fenced-in yard and hundreds of acres of forest where their pups can be trained to track a scent, the Masons had the perfect set up.

Although their work was tiring and sometimes exasperating, the Masons loved their life.

"No two people are more suited to each other," Prudie Mason liked to remind her husband every night when she turned out the lights and snuggled next to him in bed. And suited they were.

It began with their hair, but didn't end there. Mrs. Mason's hair was black as night, with highlights of tan around her ears and along the part that runs straight up from her nose. Come to think of it, Mrs. Mason's hair was the same colors as Flirt's – the champion bloodhound whose litter of ten pups they were now training. Mr. Mason's hair was mostly chocolate, with patches of butterscotch outlining his forehead and tracing his ears. He and Gotcha, the sire of the little pups, could be identical twins if he was a dog.

Not only did their hair match the coloring of their champion bloodhounds, the Masons walked in a Bloodhound-esque manner, hunched forward, noses aimed toward the ground, a trait that comes from years of training their pups to be the best in the business. And they were!

When asked how Royal Scent Kennels was able to deliver such well-trained puppies not yet three months old, Mr. Mason usually answered, "Dunno, maybe they just like music!" This odd answer prompted up a need for explanation.

Every night after dinner and doing the dishes, the Masons went out to the barn to check on their bloodhounds before going to bed. As was his practice, Mr. Mason brought along his guitar. While Mrs. Mason straightened out the dog beds, Mr. Mason saw to it that they all had plenty of fresh water and little toys to snuggle up with. When the Masons were satisfied that the dogs would be comfortable for the night, it would be time to sing them a lullaby. And sing, they did!

Sitting on a bale of hay, the Masons would face their dogs, open their mouths wide and then warm up their vocal chords by singing the scale.

"Do-re-me-fa-so-la-ti-do"

Then, after strumming three bars of music, Mr. Mason would turn to his wife, arch his furry eyebrows and lead her into their song – "You Cain't Hide From Me" – the Royal Scent Kennels training hymn.

Over the mountain, across the sea
Try as you might, you cain't hide from me
Just one long sniff and you're mine all mine
Cause it's my job to find, find, find

So lookout, baby, cause I'm gonna getcha
I'm gonna getcha, I'm gonna getcha
Just one whiff and I'm gonna getcha
You cain't hide from me!
Aw-woof! Aw-woof!
No, you cain't hide from me.

This was Flirt and Gotcha's favorite song, if it's possible for dogs to have a favorite song. Together, they would bay along with the Masons. Between the Masons singing off key and the lusty cries of the dogs, the sound was indescribable. If you happened to be going by the barn during their concert, you'd think something or someone was being tortured.

Before going to bed, the Masons always caught the eleven o'clock news. This night, a popular reporter from a Boston television station who had visited the kennel recently was doing her segment on Royal Scent Kennels.

"Nothing looks funnier than a litter of baby bloodhounds," she purred.

"Aw, here we go," Mr. Mason moaned.

"With their long ears, round bellies and deep-set eyes they look, well, goofy. In fact, their eyes are sunken so deeply in their heads that it's a wonder they can see!" The reporter began to giggle.

"Beauty is in the eye of the beholder," Mrs. Mason snapped at the TV.

"That's right. That foolish woman should have stayed long enough to see how smart they are when we put them through their paces," Mr. Mason agreed.

Mr. Mason clicked off the television and turned to his wife.

"Pucker up, Prudie girl," he flirted, as he had for the forty-odd years of their marriage. And with her lips in an

8

impressive pucker, Prudie received her husband's good night smooch. A quick scratch behind each other's ears, followed by a mutual pat on the head and it was time to burrow under a double down comforter. Lights out.

As the Masons snored peacefully, their bedroom was bathed in moonlight made brighter as it reflected from the snow-covered meadows surrounding their home. From its branch on a towering pine near the house, an owl hooted while a strong Northeast wind rattled the windowpanes, a reminder of winter to come.

In the kennel building, Flirt and her puppies snuggled deeper into a pile of old quilts, while Gotcha stayed in his own bed, always alert, until he was satisfied that his brood was settled for the night. As for the unusual little puppy that was giving everyone so much trouble, she lay stretched out on her back, her eyes focused on the barn's skylight, where she could see a million stars in the ink-black sky.

As she was about to drift off to sleep, a blazingly bright shooting star seemed to stall for a fraction of a second right over her head before whizzing by. When she blinked her eyes, it was gone.

2
School Days

~

After devouring a bowl of hot oatmeal doused with a generous shake of cinnamon, a drizzle of maple syrup and a fistful of slivered almonds, Mr. Mason rounded up the puppies for their daily training.

"Sit," Mr. Mason said firmly, giving the easiest of commands. Then, with military precision, all of the puppies, with the exception of one, did exactly as they were told. The little pocketbook chewer did a somersault, and then looked at Mr. Mason for praise. It was not forthcoming.

Next, the puppies were allowed to wander freely, taking their pick from the many toys scattered across the yard. "Leave it," Mr. Mason commanded, and all of the pups obediently dropped their toys. Except the same puppy that didn't obey "Sit" used this as an opportunity to roll over and wait for a belly scratch. When that didn't pay off she decided to try out her legs that had begun to feel as if she had springs inside. The pup had been leaping over her littermates for the past week, reaching heights that were unbelievable unless you happened to be watching. Brazenly, she decided to try to leap over her mother. Her attempt was not only unsuccessful, it earned her a hard swat from her mother's paw.

Oh well, she thought. Ma*ybe if I run faster and then jump …*

Mrs. Mason was busy writing down a description of each puppy's first choice among the toys. This was important because they would use the pup's favorite toy in their training.

Mr. Mason turned to his wife while pointing his finger at the naughty puppy. "We've got work to do, Prudie." He shook his head in frustration, his earlobes flapping back and forth.

"Listen here," he said to the errant pup, "as soon as you and your littermates are sold, Mrs. Mason and I are leaving for Florida to thaw out our bones."

The puppy cocked her head, then frowned so hard that her eyes disappeared under folds of skin.

"Seriously, we'll be sitting under our beach umbrella reading magazines while you guys are hard at work finding lost people and solving crimes." Mr. Mason picked up the puppy and held her in front of his face. He stared at her, making sure she paid attention.

"You've got to get with it, Missy. And make it fast."

After the puppies had been fed and awakened from their afternoon naps, their training continued. "Now for the serious stuff," Mrs. Mason said, her nostrils twitching in anticipation. After taking them from the kennel one-at-a-time, she held up the dog's favorite toy and let it play with it for a few minutes. Then, after harnessing the puppy and holding tight to a leash, she gave the toy to Mr. Mason who ran to hide behind the barn.

As the puppy's excitement built, she waited for Mr. Mason's call that he was ready.

"TRACK!" she yelled. Bam! The puppy scrambled around the yard until picking up the scent, then tracked directly to Mr. Mason. When he was found – actually when the *toy* was found – the puppy was given the toy as its reward. This first step was crucial in determining if the bloodhound would be a good tracker.

"How many are left?" Mr. Mason asked as he returned from behind the barn.

"Only one," Mrs. Mason answered, her eyes darting around the yard looking for you-know-who. When she couldn't find the missing puppy in the yard she went into the barn.

"PRUDIE!" Mr. Mason yelled. "Where is that little rascal?"

Out of breath, Mrs. Mason answered, "She's with me."

Instead of waiting her turn with her littermates, the troublesome little female had found a basket of freshly folded laundry under the clothesline near the barn. She was happily dragging Mr. Mason's pajamas around, stopping only to sneeze.

"LEAVE IT," Mrs. Mason said crisply in her firmest voice. Surprised, the puppy dropped the pajamas, only to go into the favorite toy basket where she snatched a squeaky stuffed lobster toy and ran in circles around Mrs. Mason. She slowed down only to trip over her feet that appear to be too large for her little body.

After rejoining his wife, Mr. Mason was clearly concerned. "This is the first time I've seen this type of behavior in one of our bloodhounds. Could it be that the puppy, is, um... not very smart?"

"It happens," Mrs. Mason answered quietly, agreeing with her husband, "just not to one of ours."

It's fair to say that bloodhound puppies are funny looking. Yet this puppy had a look that could be best described as hilarious. She was the chubbiest of the litter, with the wobbliest legs and an uncooperative tail that kept kinking up when it should have wagged. With her sneezing and general misbehavior, she'd become a cause for the Masons to be concerned. Their bloodhounds had to measure up, be the best – or the reputation of Royal Scent Kennels could be ruined.

Sensing the Masons' displeasure, the puppy shuffled back to her mother. Flirt nudged the little pup to try again. In the way that dogs communicate, Flirt beamed a thought to her pup — *It feels good to be a bloodhound.* The pup heeked, then lowered her head. It was just too hard with her sneezing. With one more nudge from Flirt, the puppy wobbled and swayed over to Mrs. Mason. Cautiously, she took a long whiff of the toy lobster.

"Good dog," Mrs. Mason praised, hopeful that the pup had caught on at last. "SIT," Mrs. Mason commanded and wow – the pup sat!!! "Good dog," Mrs. Mason praised again. *Oh, yeah.*

"Now, let's put on your harness," Mrs. Mason said, bending down. The pup wagged her tail, it felt so good to be praised. *I think I have it!* the pup thought. And then, *oh, no, here it comes – ah-, ah-, ah-choo!* When she sneezed, she tripped over her ears, tumbled over and landed on her back! Her littermates heeked a dog laugh and began imitating her, making her feel terrible.

Ashamed and deeply embarrassed, she tried to run between her father's legs for safety and security. But oops, she missed – and knocked Gotcha, a stern looking, famous crime-solving bloodhound, smack into Mr. Mason. If that wasn't bad enough, almost in slow motion, Mr. Mason lost his balance and fell hard, landing in a huge bag of dog food that rained all over the yard. Knowing that trouble was brewing, Flirt and all her puppies ran for cover.

When Gotcha got back on his feet, he looked mean and hard at his puppy. He had mistaken the pup's run for cover between his legs as an act of aggression and now he was MAD! With great effort, considering the heavy folds on his face, he raised his top lip and showed his teeth to the pup. Silence. Nobody moved, not Flirt, not the littermates – not even the Masons. The pup cocked her head to the side. *He's smiling at me,* she thought mistakenly. *Maybe I should do it again?*

Locking eyes with her famous father, the pup backed up slowly. Just then, a jet plane from a nearby air base streaked low overhead. The deafening roar prevented the pup from hearing the long, low rumble of Gotcha's warning growl. Instead, the pup bolted forward at full speed and slammed sideways into Gotcha, knocking the big guy off his feet AGAIN!

"Aren't you the *daring* one?" Mrs. Mason tittered, scooping up the pup before Gotcha could give it a swat. "We should name you Daring!"

"Hey, *Daring Dog,*" Mr. Mason said as he swept up the spilled food, a perplexed look on his face. "What am I going to do with you? If you don't track, I can't sell you and if I can't sell you, I can't keep you, and if I can't keep you I'll have to find a home for you. So you need to get with the program, understand?"

The little pup sneezed so hard that she fell out of Mrs. Mason's hands, did a somersault, and then landed spread-eagled on a pile of straw. After pulling herself back onto her feet, she bounced! *Achoo! Ah-bounce! Achoo! Ah-ah-ah-bounce!* And this time she got some attention. Gotcha tilted his head, first to the left, then to the right. At best, Gotcha was confused. How could this gangly pup come from a litter that he had sired?

As for the Masons, well, they just stood shaking their heads from side to side. Then they looked at each other in disbelief. Did that little puppy just jump about five feet off the ground?

Naw. Couldn't be.

3
What About Me???

~

When the pups were four months old and the Masons felt confident about their training, they posted their announcement of a ready-to-go litter on Facebook. On a date designated by the Masons, anxious buyers arrived to choose their pups.

Mr. Mason dressed in his best suit for the occasion. He had chosen fresh trails for the bloodhounds to track, demonstrating their training, agility and great breeding. Each puppy was put through the paces, obediently following a scent until making their find. Watching from their chairs alongside the yard, prospective buyers "oohed" and "ahhed" over the incredible tracking ability of each puppy.

When it was Daring's turn, Mr. Mason said, "We call this little girl Daring because she is fearless. Because of that, it is taking a bit longer for us to train her, but let's give her a chance today, anyway."

Mrs. Mason looked sternly at Daring, then placed her lobster toy under her nose. Daring took a big sniff. *Don't sneeze*, Mrs. Mason prayed. And she didn't. Daring sat patiently and waited for her harness to be put on and for Mrs. Mason to give the command to track. To give Daring a break, Mr. Mason hid behind the barn – the easiest place for Daring to find him.

When Mrs. Mason yelled, "track" Daring dropped her nose to the ground and took off – in the wrong direction. Instead of heading for a trail, she made a beeline for the crowd of prospective buyers, slid to a stop and then, no matter how hard she tried not to, Daring let out the biggest ACH-OO ever to come from a dog her size. It's powerful spray shot enough snot to land on three or four prospective buyers.

"We think we're going to keep this one," Mr. Mason apologized, his face growing redder by the minute.

"I'll take her from you, Doug," Mrs. Mason said, hurrying to the barn with the dejected puppy in her arms.

As the afternoon wore on, Daring watched sadly as buyers left with her littermates. She wanted to be a good bloodhound, but she just couldn't seem to measure up. Once the Masons realized that there would be no buyers for Daring, Mr. Mason began to pace back and forth in the yard. Flirt and Gotcha, who always preened and puffed themselves up proudly when their prized offspring were bought, were mortified, too embarrassed to even look at Daring.

"We've got to get rid of her," Mr. Mason told his wife. "I don't want to have to drive all the way to Florida with that puppy in the van. My sister's being generous enough to take care of Flirt and Gotcha for the winter. We can't stick her with the pup, too."

Reluctantly, Mrs. Mason agreed. She scratched her head and rubbed her chin vigorously. "I've got it! Let's put a sign out on the highway."

"It's worth a try," Mr. Mason agreed as he got out a piece of wood and some black paint.

BLOODHOUND PUPPY - ONLY ONE LEFT
HALF PRICE

A few hours later, a Maine State Trooper happened to be passing by. Once he read the sign, he slammed on his brakes, coming to a screeching stop. *Did the sign really read half price for a Royal Scent bloodhound,* he wondered. *That is an incredible deal!* He turned his squad car around and headed down the long, bumpy road.

Upon hearing the approaching vehicle, the Masons gathered up Daring and stood proudly by her side. "Be smart," Mr. Mason warned the pup. Daring understood. She stood with her head lowered, heart pounding. The trooper had a kind face and a soft voice. *Please take me,* she wished.

"Why the discount?" the trooper asked as he exited the squad car. "Everyone knows that these are the best bloodhounds in the country."

"Then you know our dogs," Mrs. Mason said proudly, trying not to show her nervousness.

"Yes, ma'am. I sure do and I would love to have one." The trooper spotted Daring who looked up at him with her hopeful, sweet brown eyes.

"Hey there, cutie," The trooper patted the crown of her head, then scratched behind her ear. Daring leaned into his big hand. *Oh that felt good!*

"Ah-hem!" Mr. Mason cleared his throat while willing Daring not to do something foolish. "To be honest, this little gal has good days and some that need improvement, but she's from great parents." Mr. Mason gestured toward Flirt and Gotcha who pretended to ignore the conversation. "She just needs a lot of attention to get her going."

The trooper continued to pat Daring. She looked up at him. *Please take me,* she begged with her eyes. When she lapped his hand in a bloodhound kiss, the deal was done.

19

"Sold," he announced, while handing over his credit card.

Daring's heart soared as she leaped into the back seat of the patrol car, proud that she was going to be a genuine crime-solving bloodhound. Or so she thought.

⤸

The following Monday, the Masons were packing up and ready to go south for the winter, when a car peeled down their driveway. It was the trooper.

"Uh, oh," Mr. Mason murmured.

"No surprise," Mrs. Mason said forlornly.

The trooper jumped out of the patrol car, red-faced and furious. In a second, he opened the rear door and nudged a humiliated Daring from the back seat.

"This dog couldn't find her own nose!" the trooper complained. Mrs. Mason gave her husband a knowing look. They were afraid of this.

"Watch this," the trooper said, as he took off his shirt to reveal a big belly covered by a huge tattoo of a cow. He threw the shirt to Mr. Mason. "Now you hold onto her while I go behind your barn."

Mr. Mason took Daring's collar. "You can do it, Daring," she prayed, "you're a good dog."

In a minute, the trooper yelled, "I'm ready." Mr. Mason bent down and went nose to nose with Daring. "TRACK!," he yelled.

Daring put her nose to the shirt, took a long, heartfelt sniff, and then looked at Mr. Mason and ... *Achoo!* She sneezed so hard that she bounced almost as high as Mr. Mason's shoulders, covering him with spray as she landed. Mr. Mason seethed, but Daring was undaunted. Next,

Daring sniffed around Mrs. Mason until finally she stopped at Mrs. Mason's feet, looked up and offered a weak heek.

"What did I tell you?" the trooper ranted when he returned from behind the barn. "I want my money back."

"That's no problem," Mr. Mason said, "I'll credit your charge card, if you give me a minute."

While waiting for Mr. Mason to return, the trooper bent down to scratch Daring behind the ear. "Sorry girl, you're a real cutie but you haven't got the right stuff." Daring wished she could sink into the ground.

After the trooper drove off, Mrs. Mason looked at her husband, then to the sorry-looking puppy. "It looks like we'll have company in Florida," she said quietly. Reluctantly, Mr. Mason nodded in agreement.

Daring began to cry. "Heek, heek, heek." The creases in her forehead deepened and her tears mapped a crooked trail down her cheeks. More than anything on earth she wanted to make her parents and the Masons proud. She *wanted* to catch criminals. She was *born* to catch criminals. If only she'd had the chance.

A few days later, Mr. Mason's sister, Peggy, a spritely woman with a kind voice and a quick step, arrived to take Flirt and Gotcha to spend the winter with her at her lakeside home. When the dogs were called to come to her car, Daring followed eagerly.

"Not you, Daring," Mrs. Mason said, although a note of wishful thinking could be detected in the tone of her voice.

"We're always grateful, Peg," Mr. Mason said as he loaded the dogs' beds and bags of food into the trunk of her car.

"No problem, Doug. They're good company when the storms get going and I'm stuck inside," Peggy said. "Have a good winter!"

Daring watched sadly as Peggy's car drove off. *Why am I here all by myself,* she wondered.

❧

At daybreak, Mr. Mason did a final check of his property, careful to lock all windows and doors and to store in the barn anything that could be blown away by a fierce Northeast storm.

After cramming a little dog bed, a few toys, food and water bowls into the van, Mr. Mason went back to fetch his wife. Standing in the doorway, a big grin on his face, he removed his thick, wool hat and replaced it with his Boston Red Sox World Series cap.

"I've warmed up the van and we're good to go. Are we ready, my dearest Prudence?"

"Ready, willing and able," she answered, giving him an affectionate squeeze.

After settling Daring into her spot, they slid into their seats, buckled their seatbelts, adjusted the heater, and then drove down their snow-covered driveway, thrilled to begin the long drive from downeast Maine to their neat little trailer in the Florida Keys.

At the end of their driveway they craned their necks to take one last look back at Royal Scent Kennels. Satisfied that all was in order and buttoned up tight, Doug and Prudie Mason began to sing their traveling-to-Florida song.

"*...Off the Florida Keys, there's a place called Kokomo...*" When Daring began slapping her tail to the beat of their song, Mrs. Mason reached behind her to pat the pup. *Wow, I really am special,* Daring thought. *I have a soft bed and something to chew on. I think they're happy to keep me.* Yeah, right.

4
Shorty's Diner, Port Oscar, Maine

~

Seven a.m.

As was their habit, once on the road, the Masons made their first stop at a local coffee shop where they always ordered homemade muffins and filled their thermos with Shorty's special blend coffee. As they decided between blueberry peach and cranberry walnut muffins, they had the misfortune of passing by Cade Walker, a local high school dropout who has had more than one tussle with the law.

Unlike most kids his age who dressed more or less alike in the fashion of the day, Cade dressed like a cowboy even though it's doubtful that he'd ever been on a horse. Instead, he watched Western movies, and wouldn't you know it – he always cheered for the bad guys. In fact, his screen name was "Maine'sBaddestDude".

Cade wore cowboy boots with sharp silver tips on the toes. A silver studded hatband was wrapped around his Stetson hat. His belt was nothing more than thick silver chains, held together with a mean looking buckle shaped like the head of a fang-baring snake. With Cade's flashing eyes, the stubbly beard he was trying to grow, and the turned down corners of his mouth, he looked like an angry, vicious Rottweiler.

Cade had bought his coffee and was about to climb into his truck when he noticed the Royal Scent Kennel sign that was painted on the Masons' van door. It read "Champion Bloodhounds". When Cade saw the open window that Mrs. Mason had left for Daring to get fresh air, he looked around to see who might be watching, and then sauntered over to the van and peered in. *These champion bloodhounds are worth a fortune,* he thought. *Today's my lucky day.* First, he checked to be sure the Masons were still inside the coffee shop, and then with one quick swipe, he reached in, unlocked the door – and snatched Daring.

"Yippee-ky-yo! Hey little guy, meet your new owner!" Cade lifted his cowboy hat as if to salute Daring, then threw his truck into gear and raced out of the parking lot. Daring eyed Cade warily. Her bloodhound nose smelled trouble.

As soon as Cade returned home, he lifted the pup out of the truck and put her on the gravel driveway where Daring squatted to do her business. Seeing the puppy skootch down instead of lifting a hind leg, Cade lifted up her tail. "Oh great, you ain't a guy!" *Already he doesn't like me,* Daring thought when she heard his tone. And as if to seal the deal, suddenly, Daring sneezed so hard that she sprayed Cade with her snot.

"Gross!" Cade groaned, using his sleeve to wipe Daring's snot from his face. Finally, he noticed her tag and took time to read it. "Daring, huh? We'll see about that!"

When the Masons returned to their van, they were shocked to see that Daring was not where they left her.

"Look in the back," Mr. Mason suggested. "Maybe she's gotten into something – it would be just like her," he snitted.

"She's gone!" Mrs. Mason shrieked after a frantic search in and around the van. "We have to look for her, Doug. She'll freeze out here in the cold!" Without much enthusiasm, Mr. Mason agreed. "That dog was nothing but trouble since the day she was born." Still, he loved animals and knew the puppy could come to harm ... or someone had stolen her from the van.

After searching for almost an hour, calling her name, looking behind buildings and in bushes, the Masons realized that Daring was most likely gone for good. "I'll leave my cell phone number in Shorty's in case someone finds her," Mr. Mason said. "What else can we do?"

"We have to notify the police, Doug. She's just a pup, for goodness sake."

"You're right," he fretted. "The station's just around the corner."

After filing a report for the missing puppy, Mr. Mason returned to their van.

"I guess that's it then," he said, climbing back into the van. "I know you're upset, Pru, but face it – she never had much luck as one of our bloodhounds. I'm sure that someone will find her and take her in as a pet."

"Let's hope," Mrs. Mason said softly. Then she closed her eyes and said a little prayer for Daring Dog, just four months old.

With Daring in tow, Cade opened the squeaky door to his grandmother's now-vacant summer cottage, where he'd been living after his bad behavior got to be too much for his parents to handle. The table and counters were littered with dirty dishes and half-eaten frozen dinners.

Cade opened the refrigerator and reached for a can of soda. After a long burp, Cade took a good look at Daring. "I suppose you want some grub?"

Daring looked up at him, tilted her head to the side and heeked.

"Don't be whining at me," Cade warned her. He dropped a cracker on the floor in front of Daring and then filled a bowl with water.

Daring gobbled the cracker and drank hungrily, but Cade's meager offering didn't satisfy her need for a meal. She was a growing pup, after all. Daring looked up at Cade hopefully until he went back to the refrigerator and threw a slice of cheese her way. "That's it, kiddo," Cade said. He'd have to buy some dog food in the morning.

Feeling a little better, Daring settled on a pile of his unwashed laundry. She was about to take a nap when Cade said, "I was thinking I could sell you on eBay and make a quick buck, but maybe I'll keep you and train you – then you'll be worth a heckuva lot more." Cade thought, *maybe I could even get enough money to move down south – or even to California.*"

Daring was clueless as to what Cade was saying, but she wagged her tail to please him. He was, after all, in charge of the food. Or so it seemed.

5

One Year Later – All Grown Up

~

Winter melted into spring; spring blossomed into summer and summer faded into fall. Cade's grandmother had fallen ill and frail, and was never able to return to her cottage. Ever the doting grandmother, she'd told Cade's parents, "Let Cade stay there, he's a good boy," despite their efforts to convince her to make him move out, get a job and be responsible for himself.

As the seasons changed, Daring's sneezing got worse. She sniffled, sneezed harder and bounced even higher. Sadly, there were days when she was left outside with nothing but an old shoe to toss around. Bored silly and sneezing often, sometimes she entertained herself by bouncing almost to the roof of the cottage. Now, fully grown despite poor nutrition, she was bony and thin, even funnier looking than when she was a pup. The kink in her tail had grown longer as she'd grown larger. Now it bent at a right angle, looking more like an airplane rudder than a bloodhound's tail.

Cade and Daring had settled into a miserable existence. Poor Daring was always hungry, while Cade was always angry and bored. Days and nights were spent watching endless

Western movies. The only time Cade went out was to steal something that he could sell for food and gas money. There were moments when Cade thought he'd like to get a job, but he believed no one would hire him since he was a high school drop out. The only job he'd ever had was for his grandmother's neighbor who'd paid him to do odd jobs, like mowing the lawn and shoveling snow. Truth be told, he'd stolen a few dollars from her pocketbook when she wasn't looking. Needless to say, he wasn't asked back after his theft was discovered.

With nothing but time on his hands, it was too bad that Cade thought that reading books was for dummies. His grandmother's den was filled with bookcases crammed with a variety of books on almost every topic. In fact, there were a fair number of books about the Wild West that you would think would entice Cade to at least look at a few pages. But no matter how many times Cade passed by a shelf lined with books that were bound to interest him, he paid no attention.

Now, almost a year to the day when he had stolen Daring, Cade decided that it was time to follow through with his original plan. *Purebred bloodhounds are worth moo-lah,* he had thought when he first spied her in the Masons' van. Now it was time sell the bloodhound and get enough money to hit the road to Cal-i-forn-i-a.

Suddenly, it dawned on Cade that Daring would be worth a lot more if he could demonstrate what a good tracker she was.

"I'll have to train you, I guess," he told Daring. "I just have to figure out how."

Cade searched YouTube until he found a bloodhound training video. With his lack of patience and know-it-all attitude, Cade fast-forwarded the video until he thought he knew what to do.

"You stay here," he told Daring, leaving the dog in the cottage while he went outside to hide one of his well worn, rarely washed socks. *I'll teach her to track in no time,* he thought.

When he returned to Daring, he took another of his dirty socks and held it under her nose. No harness, no favorite toy that she was attached to, nothing – Cade had skipped the basics. Instead, he just screamed in Daring's face – "TRACK, DARING"!

Daring didn't move.

Again, this time louder, Cade demanded, "TRAAAACK!"

The dog looked at Cade. Clearly, she understood him, but instead of tracking, Daring flattened her body on the floor, her front paws covering her nose! Disgusted, Cade berated her. "You are one useless dog. No supper for you tonight!"

Daring flopped her head down, tried to stifle a sneeze, but ended up sneezing harder than ever, shooting snot spray in Cade's direction. "You're useless, you dumb dog," he screamed. Furious, Cade swatted her hard with a rolled up newspaper as she cowered on the floor. If that wasn't enough, he dragged her by her fur and then chained her to a rotted tree trunk outside the back door. Hours later, when Cade finally brought her inside, Daring was covered with snow, shivering hard, nearly frozen to death.

Once he calmed down, Cade realized that although he hadn't been able to train her to track, Daring was still worth a lot of money since she came from champion bloodhound stock. *Maybe I'll just clean her up and sell her,* he considered.

6

Welcome To
Misty Harbor, Maine
Est. 1797

~

Misty Harbor, Maine is the kind of town that most kids would love to grow up in.

There were large playgrounds, challenging skateboard parks, and wide bike lanes that laced through the small town. During the summer, people who loved to sail could be found at Sailor's Landing, where many residents tied up their boats. At Sandy Lane Beach, families enjoyed one of the few soft sand beaches in the area, making it a great place for picnics and swimming during the glorious, but short, Maine summer. With whale watching becoming a popular tourist attraction, scientists from the Coastal Learning Center gave lectures about whales, porpoises and other ocean inhabitants that lived in local waters. In the fall, kids walked to school over a carpet of maple and oak leaves turned deep ruby red and golden yellow – a riot of color, crunching under foot.

On weekends, much of the townspeople turned out for rowdy football games at the local high school field. Farm stands sagged with the harvest of squash and pumpkins, corn and tomatoes. On weekends, people came from miles around to enjoy a hayride through the local apple orchard, followed by homemade donuts, and a cup of fresh apple cider. When kids got hungry they could go down to the pier, where they could eat foot-long hot dogs. Or they could dive right into a delicious pizza with every different kind of topping you could imagine – even lobster!

When winter arrived, this active community spent hours at the skating rink, or racing down twisty toboggan runs, or going cross country skiing through the hiking trails that wound through pine forests on the edge of town.

You might think that Misty Harbor sounds a bit old-fashioned, and in some ways you'd be right. Everything one could need was just about around the corner! Plus, with the arrival of Internet service, many people were able to work at home with the world at their fingertips. They could Google, email, text and tweet to their hearts' content. Yes, Misty Harbor, Maine was a cool place to live.

However, no town is *perfect*. Instead of the big city sounds, smog, and congestion to make life irritating, Misty Harbor had a sardine factory where Maine's Supreme Sardines were prepared for shipment all over the world. This business was good for the town and provided many jobs – but when the wind blew from east to west, the smell from the factory was so strong that people held their noses and shut their windows, even on the hottest summer days. Still, that was the only downside about living in this beautiful village on Maine's rockbound coast.

Just last year, *Coastal America Magazine* named Misty Harbor one of the most idyllic villages in Maine, with a crime rate that was practically zero. Everything was so peaceful in Misty Harbor that people rarely locked their doors. Other than some nuisance calls once in awhile, the police force had nothing much to do except drive around town, munching on homemade goodies from the Nor'easter Natural Food Store. So it was about the worst thing that could happen when Cade Walker, looking for new neighborhoods to steal from, decided to expand his territory and target the unsuspecting citizens of Misty Harbor.

7

Misty Harbor Lighthouse

～

Sam Harris, a technology geek, aspiring sleuth and serious filmmaker, was hard at work on his computer editing a YouTube video about a missing cat, the treasured companion of Gladys Grady, an eccentric elderly lady known for her apple pies and her ability to read palms.

"I can read your palm and tell you your future, but I can't read my own so what good is it?" Mrs. Grady lamented. "I need to know if I will ever find Prince Charming," she'd told Sam after learning that he was a whiz on the computer. "Is there any way you can help me?" the distraught woman pleaded. Mrs. Grady worked as a volunteer at the hospital where Sam had his physical therapy.

With a little encouragement from his father, Sam agreed. "Bring me some pictures of the cat and I'll see what I can do," he told her.

Gladys Grady arrived at Sam's front door a few hours later carrying a sack full of photos of her cat and a freshly baked apple pie. "I can't pay you much," she said, "but I can read your palm and tell you your future."

"No thank you," said Sam. He didn't want to know if bad luck would follow him in the years ahead. He'd already had more than his share.

As Sam scanned the photos, his father finished fixing a leaking faucet in the kitchen sink. After putting his tools away, Mr. Harris continued with his squeaky attempts at yodeling, a practice he'd picked up when, as a child, he attended summer camp in Tennessee's Great Smokey Mountains. He was so bad a yodeler, and made such annoying squeaks that it drove his son crazy.

"Dad, please! I can't concentrate," Sam grumped.

"Sorry about that," his father apologized.

"Why don't you yodel in the lighthouse?" Sam suggested, "It sounds better in there."

Sam and his father lived in a small, white house that was attached to the Misty Harbor Lighthouse. The buildings, along with a small boathouse, perched atop a breakwater built of jagged rocks that was connected to the mainland by a narrow road nearly a half a mile long. On days when the ocean was calm, it was an easy walk or drive to the mainland. But when the sea was rough, powerful waves often crashed over the breakwater. Sometimes the waves were so high that it was too dangerous to leave the house.

In addition to making videos, Sam spent a lot of time on his computer, or playing with his other high tech gadgets. He had a tablet, a laptop computer, two monitors, movie-making and editing software, scanners, printers, wireless webcams, and even a police band radio. There were other gizmos in his room as well, including antennas and weird looking communications things that Mr. Harris had brought to him from the Media Lab.

Mr. Harris had also taught Sam how to write computer programs to direct Archie, a six-foot tall, stainless steel robot that Mr. Harris had built to do chores and run the house while Sam was recuperating from the accident. Mr. Harris was careful to include parental controls that only he could access, despite his clever son's ability to write software.

Sam could spend hours working at his computers, and had found movie-making to be something he was getting quite good at. He was at a point in his movie where Mrs. Grady was pleading for help in finding her cat.

"Prince Charming is my best friend – ayuh," she explained in her crackled, voice with her thick Maine accent. "We watch television togeth-ah every night and he follows me every-way-ah." Mrs. Grady struggled to hold back her tears. "I'm sick with worry, I don't know what I will do without him. If somebody has him please bring him home." Mrs. Grady then lost her composure and began to sob. She gestured for the camera to stop filming.

Right then, Sam's father entered the room carrying a snack of apple slices and peanut butter. "How's it going, Sam?"

"All right, I'm adding some special effects right now, and then I'll put this part up on YouTube tonight. I feel sorry for her, Dad, Mrs. Grady's really losing it."

"Well, maybe your video will do the trick," his father hoped.

"I've been tweeting my school list and it's like no one cares," Sam worried. "You should read some of tweets I get back. Some of them are really mean, like one kid tweeted that he ate the cat for supper! Kids in this town are weird."

"People can be very self-involved, Sam."

"But this old lady – the cat is all she has. You know what I think, Dad? It's better not to have a pet – then you won't be sorry when you lose it. Look at Mrs. Grady, she's like crazed."

Sam looked at his father who sat stone-faced, unable to look at his son. *Will he ever come out of this?* Mr. Harris fretted. *I can design computers, build a robot, and solve the most difficult technical problems, yet I have no idea how to mend my boy's broken heart?*

Davidson Harris was a sad-eyed, stooped-over scientist who had taken a leave of absence from teaching at the Media Lab, a phantasmagoric think tank at Massachusetts Technology Institute near Boston. With his wild mop of prematurely gray hair, piercing brown eyes and bushy eyebrows that curled over his frameless glasses, he had the look and attitude of an absent-minded professor. Mr. Harris had planned to work for many more years, but the accident that took his beloved wife's life, and nearly killed his son, has changed all of that.

Instead of staying in their suburban Boston home that was filled with too many memories, and a staircase that Sam could no longer manage, Mr. Harris offered to replace the about-to-retire Misty Harbor lighthouse keeper, who just happened to be Sam's great-grandfather.

While growing up, Louise Spencer Harris had spent many fun-filled summers with her grandfather in the light-house keeper's little home. Just two summers ago, she had taken Sam to stay with her Grampy Spencer for a whole month, before continuing on to Greenland, where she had a summer research grant allowing her to study the behavior of whales. Sam had loved riding his bicycle back and forth along the bumpy breakwater road. Every morning they would pick wild Maine blueberries for their breakfast cereal and sometimes Louise would whip up a batch of blueberry muffins from an old recipe that Nana Spencer had given to her. Although Sam didn't know any of the local kids, except for the few he would see in the ice cream shop or when they went for groceries, he was happy and content to spend hours collecting rocks, following the antics of passing seals, and playing computer games with his dad.

The decision to move to Misty Harbor seemed right at the time, but seeing his son's misery, Mr. Harris was having second thoughts. *I'll make it work, I have to,* he told himself repeatedly.

For his part, Mr. Harris had always loved Misty Harbor. For years, the only time he would agree to take a few weeks off from the Media Lab would be to spend time with his family and Louise's grandfather in Misty Harbor. In fact, the WELLBEENER – the transparent biometric checking wristband he invented – was imagined during a visit to Misty Harbor. His wonderful invention was a boon to checking the blood pressure and pulse of patients of all ages.

Mr. Harris's absolute favorite thing about Misty Harbor was the lighthouse, itself, its round shape and stone walls a perfect stage for him to pursue his unusual hobby – yodeling. In the lighthouse, one string of yodels reverberated as if it were the best Dolby sound system. Unfortunately, Mr. Harris didn't have much to yodel about any more. On the rare occasion that he tried to yodel, his throat closed up and he was barely able to croak.

Although Mr. Harris had taken great care to make their house comfortable and easy for Sam to navigate in his wheelchair, the boy was miserable. Sam hated being in a wheelchair, looked for excuses to miss school, and he barely ate the scrumptious meals that Archie prepared. Instead, he remained inside the house despite invitations from kids whom Sam believed were being forced by their parents to invite him over. Only Lily Cohen, a red-haired, freckle-faced, whisper of a girl with a toothy grin, who lived near the entrance to the breakwater, was able to get his attention. Lily loved working on Sam's videos and Sam appeared to enjoy her company, enough so that they texted each other every night before going to bed. Sometimes, a friendly text from Lily was enough to get Sam through the night. Other times, in the middle of the night, disturbing visions flooded back into Sam's mind.

It's so cold. I AM following your footsteps. The clouds? They're mackerel backs. What's that sound? Look at the sky. It's blue, no, it's dark, there's no light. Why are they screaming at me? Mom, Mom, Mummy! Where IS she? Who's this man? How did he get here? ...What's your name, son?

"Oh Sam, Sam," Mr. Harris whispered stroking his son's thick dark hair, trying to soothe him, "it's okay, son, just another bad dream."

Sam wiped the tears from his deep-set brown eyes and reached for the colorful hat he kept under his pillow. Then, burying his face into his mother's hat – the same hat that he had watched the wind lift off her head a second before it happened – he slid deeper under the quilts until he fell asleep, his worried father in a chair by his side.

8
An Unwelcome Visitor
~

Meanwhile, as the citizens of Misty Harbor slept, Cade sneaked into town. After cruising down a few streets in a section of town where there weren't many street lamps, he chose a house surrounded by high bushes, an easy place to hide if he needed to. The only light on in the house came from a digital clock on a table in the front hall. The time read 1:59 a.m. Cade had decided to hide behind a bush closest to the front door. When he was convinced there was not a peep coming from the house, he got up slowly, only to be stabbed by a sharp thorn from the rose bush he'd chosen for cover.

"*Dang*," he muttered. Then he wiggled his way free, looked around to be sure the coast was clear, and then started for the front steps. When he hit the first step, it creaked. Cade didn't move. Nervous, he cocked his head to listen for any sound coming from the house. Silence. He continued to the front door, turned the doorknob carefully and found the door unlocked. With one quick twist of the knob, he was inside.

It's like taking candy from a baby, Cade thought as he loaded up the truck with a laptop computer, an iNotepad, and a small flat screen television.

Buoyed by his easy score, Cade spent the next few hours hitting up houses in other neighborhoods, until he had no more room in his truck to carry his stolen goods. He couldn't wait to get on his computer to determine a good price for his loot and then start selling his loot online.

The next day, when the town awakened, people were shocked and confused. "Who would do such a thing?" they wondered aloud.

"When was the last time you've had something like this happen in Misty Harbor?" asked a television news reporter.

"Never," Chief Butters bellowed. "I'll tell you something, right now. If the guys who did this are watching, well, you better watch out. Meanwhile, I want everyone on the lookout. Call the station if you see anyone suspicious." The Chief began punching his right fist into his left palm to show how serious he was. "For now, I'm asking you to lock your doors at night, at least until we catch the crooks," he continued. Chief Butters took a long pause, adjusted his holster and stared into the camera, summoning up the toughest expression he knew. "As for you guys, if you're watching – we're coming to getcha and when we do, you'll be sorry." Butters' face reddened, sweat broke out on his brow. His nostrils widened as he puffed himself up to be as large as he could be.

Meanwhile, Cade was already at work erasing the contents of the hard drive on the laptop computer he had scored. "Ain't I just awful?" he mocked to his new smart TV set that used to be in the home of an elderly man whose only joy was to watch old movies with the sound cranked way up high.

"Hey, Daring, your old man's famous!" Cade said as he scratched his unwashed head.

Daring was curled up in a corner, as far away as she could get from Cade. She hunched down as Cade came closer, waiting for the inevitable whack he usually landed on her head. If Cade wasn't slapping her head, he was tugging her ears or yanking her crooked tail. Cade was a poster boy for animal cruelty.

Since living with Cade, Daring's once shiny puppy coat had turned scruffy, her sad eyes even sadder. Cade often forgot to feed her and when he did remember it was rarely nutritious. Let's face it – a dog needs more than a handful of French fries. The only time Daring had a sparkle was when the sun hit her strands of drool in a certain way. It's no wonder that Daring slinked around without any spunk. And although he'd had her for almost a year, no owner's name or address was listed on the rusting identification tag the Masons had hung from her collar. Just her name – Daring Dog.

After Cade added up what he expected to get from selling the goods he didn't want to keep, he logged on to the Misty Harbor Chamber of Commerce website. *Let's see what's going on in that sweet little town,* he thought.

On the home page of the website he read that the Misty Harbor Hospital Women's Group was selling raffle tickets to win the latest iPad which was on display in the hospital lobby. Cade couldn't resist.

"Want to be my sidekick tomorrow?" he asked Daring. Not understanding, but responding to the excitement in Cade's voice, Daring thumped her tail. *He's smiling at me,* Daring realized. *Maybe I'm a good dog, after all.*

On the following day, Cade and Daring awakened to sunshine, made even brighter by the reflection on the nearby ocean. Cade walked outside, while Daring took her bathroom break. He inhaled a long, deep lung-full of the ocean air. *Maybe I should quit while I'm ahead, sell the stuff, take the money and hit the road. Winter in Maine sucks,* he thought. Then again, that rockin' iPad just sitting there waiting for him in the Hospital lobby would get him another easy hundred bucks, a thought he couldn't resist.

After dressing in the same outfit he'd worn for days, and eating a stale muffin washed down by a can of soda, Cade was ready to make his big score.

"Hop in fleabag," he said to Daring, who had gobbled her little breakfast too quickly and was suffering an attack of gas.

"Pee-yoo!" Cade groaned, then despite the cold wind off the ocean, he lowered both windows.

When they arrived in the parking lot behind the hospital, Cade yanked Daring's ear before he chained her to the door handle. "That's for the fart, fleabag," he said, showing her his fist.

"I'll be back in a flash." Then Cade dashed out of the truck and ran toward the hospital.

Daring had no idea why Cade was so angry with her, but she was used to it by now. *Oh well, I'll grab a quick nap, happy to be alone,* she thought.

When she was nearly asleep, her nose began to twitch and twist. *What's that smell? It's delicious!* Then Daring took another whiff, which resulted in her blasting out a big, gooey sneeze. *Acho-oo!* She didn't care. The smell from the sardine factory was overwhelming. *Food!* she thought as she began to drool! *Yum, yum, yum.*

Led by her nose, Daring peered out the window. The sun was shining, the air clean and crisp. Ah-h-h– She took a long, deep breath, as her stomach rumbled and she drooled at the thought of tasting something that smelled so wonderful. *Darn, there's that itch again!* Daring tossed her head back hard, twisted her neck, and then twisted some more until she could hit the very spot where a flea was munching on her tender skin. As she twisted harder in pursuit of the flea, she heard a – CLANK! The chain had come loose and was now resting comfortably on the floor in front of the seat. Not knowing what to do, Daring did nothing – for almost one whole minute until she started to think ...

*Wait a minute. The window is open – I can get out of here and find something to ea*t *– maybe I can TRACK MY WAY HOME!* Daring pushed her front legs out first, took a deep breath, wiggled around and with just seconds to spare, she tumbled out of the car. Free at last!

Well, almost. Her nostrils began to twitch as she caught a whiff of Cade's stinky smell as he walked toward the car. There was no time to get away. She knew she must hide! Foolishly, she slid under Cade's truck, thinking she could get away before he drove off. From beneath the chassis, her heart pounded as she watched his boots move closer. When his scent grew stronger, Daring trembled in fear. Then Cade dropped something! But true to form, he didn't pick it up. He just nonchalantly jumped into his truck, slipped the key into the ignition and was about to throw the truck into reverse when Daring decided to try to scamper out.

Unfortunately, she was stuck. Desperately, Daring tried to wriggle free, but her movement just lodged her body even more tightly. *This is it, I'm history,* she thought.

Before hitting the accelerator, Cade slipped the iPad3 out from under his jacket and stowed it under the passenger seat.

"What the devil?" he exclaimed seeing the empty seat with just the chain where Daring once sat. He was about to get out of the truck to search for the dog when he saw a security guard running into the parking lot, undoubtedly looking for him. For one last time, Daring tried to wiggle free when her feet slipped on a patch of ice. Instinctively, Daring lowered her large head. And Cade floored it – Vroom, vroom, vroom ...

And then THUMP!

His truck ran over Daring's skinny, flea-bitten, sad body. With a whimper, she laid still on the pavement, her head down, as her sad, short life flashed before her eyes. She was a goner.

Cade looked out the rear view mirror to see what the loud thump was. He saw Daring's broken body lying there. Not even the security guard noticed her. "I told you that you are a dumb dog," he yelled without even a care about the poor animal that was lying sprawled on the ground. "Just my luck," he muttered. If he was heartbroken over losing Daring, he certainly didn't show it.

9
Coastal General Hospital

~

A fter an hour of physical therapy, Sam blew out of the treatment room. It had been a frustrating, even a bit painful session and he was eager to get home.

"Why do you make me do this?" Sam confronted his father for the umpteenth time. "It doesn't work, it hurts and I hate it, Dad. And I hate you for making me do it."

"Sam, you have heard everything the doctors have said. If you don't do therapy your muscles will atrophy and the road back for you will be even longer."

"I don't want to talk about it! I hate this place, hate it, hate, hate it!" When they arrived at the elevator, a boy in Sam's class shuffled toward them. Sam tried to ignore him at first, but when it appeared that they were all waiting for the same elevator, Sam felt he had to acknowledge him.

"Hey, Basil," Sam barely mumbled.

"Yo," the kid begrudgingly grunted, and then smirked as he turned away. The elevator doors finally arrived.

"Come on, Dad," Sam said, when his father stopped pushing Sam's wheelchair to check messages on his phone.

Not another word was spoken by anyone on the short ride to the lobby.

"Who's that boy you said 'hi' to?" Mr. Harris asked. "Just because you're angry with me that is no reason to be rude and not introduce me."

"He's no one," Sam said curtly.

"No one? What's going on, Sam? Is that boy in your class?"

"I dunno," Sam shrugged off the question.

"You don't KNOW?" Mr. Harris stopped walking. "You greeted him."

Sam spun his wheelchair around to face his dad. "Yes, all right? He's in my class, his name is Basil and he's a JERK! Everyone in this place is a jerk and you should know that I HATE IT HERE!!! This is a DUMB PLACE TO LIVE. I want to go back to our house, Dad. I want to go home."

Mr. Harris nodded his head to show sympathy and understanding to his son, unsure of what to say – so he said nothing.

Sam didn't bother to tell his father that Basil Pettibone was the leader of a gang of young bullies whose main target was Sam. Nor did he tell his father about the mean texts they sent to him, the nasty tweets and how they harassed Lily for being his friend … or how they picked on him and mocked him in his wheelchair, and left smelly food in his locker. Instead, he kept it all bottled up inside eating away at him, making a sad boy even sadder.

Unfortunately for Sam, his new teacher, Mrs. Crane, hadn't realized the effect it would have on Basil and the Crabs when she had announced that a new student would be coming to their school.

"Our new classmate uses a wheelchair," she had explained. "With his special needs, it's important that we do everything to make him feel welcome."

Mrs. Crane's announcement had the opposite effect on Basil and his crew. "Fresh blood," Basil had growled to the Crabs, using a voice he'd heard in some scary movie on a television show that he wasn't allowed to watch. Together, they looked forward to picking on Sam whenever they could.

While Sam boiled inside and his dad was deep in thought, they walked out the door to the parking lot. As they made their way to their car, out of the corner of his eye, Sam saw Basil flip him the bird. Sam ignored him, even though he would have liked to smash into him with his wheelchair.

As it did most December afternoons, the wind shifted, now blowing from east to west and the smell from the factory permeated the entire town.

"Eee-you," Sam said, holding his nose.

"Oh, it's not so bad," Mr. Harris disagreed, trying to be upbeat. "Want to grab a tuna sandwich and a milkshake? It's past lunchtime and I'm starving."

"I'm going to puke, Dad," Sam said, making gagging sounds for effect.

"Well, how about a pizza, then?"

Sam nodded, but continued to hold his nose.

He raced ahead of his father, cut a 360, popped a wheelie in his wheelchair, and landed hard. Then, in the blink of an eye, his life was about to change.

"Dad, look! There's a dog lying there – and I think it's DEAD!"

Pushing his wheelchair at full speed, Sam got to Daring in time to see her struggling to move. After one valiant attempt, Daring dropped her head back and closed her eyes

"Oh my God, it's alive," Sam gasped, "I think it's been run over!" Mr. Harris ran to join his son. Together, they stared down at the poor, broken animal that was barely clinging to life.

Daring was close to dying, but when she heard the concern in Sam's voice, she opened her eyes.

"We've got to help her," Sam insisted. Mr. Harris took a deep breath, studied the dog, and then scratched the back of his head. As usual, Sam's quiet, soft-spoken father thought before he acted. Sometimes this habit of his drove Sam crazy. Like right now...

"Don't just stand there, Dad." Sam was frantic.

Mr. Harris snapped out of his thoughts.

"We shouldn't move her, son." Mr. Harris stood frozen to the spot, nervously twirling a stray piece of hair that hung on his forehead.

Sam raised his voice. "Are you kidding? If we don't move the dog, it'll get run over – again!"

Mr. Harris realized Sam was right. Without hesitating any longer, he bent down to try to lift the pathetic looking dog.

Daring groaned in pain as Mr. Harris slid his arms under her. With great effort, he lifted her up and staggered to his car. Sam held the door open as his dad slid Daring onto the back seat.

"Put me in back beside the dog," Sam insisted.

"Dr. Schnitzel's office is right around the corner," Mr. Harris said while turning the ignition. "We'll take it over there. They'll know what to do."

As they made the short drive to the veterinarian's office, Sam tried to comfort Daring, stroking her fur, careful to be gentle. He spoke softly to reassure the dog, "Hold on, buddy, you're gonna be all right." Daring did not respond.

"We're almost there," Sam said softly.

When they reached Dr. Schnitzel's office they saw a big sign hanging on the door.

CLOSED

"OH NO," Sam cried, "What about the new vet?"

Sam remembered hearing on the news about a new veterinarian who had just opened an office in a little building down by the wharf.

"Good thinking, Sam," Mr. Harris turned the car around to head across town.

And for the first time in a long while, Sam bristled with excitement.

10
Fanny Sunshine Trout, D.V.M.

~

The vet's office was located in a small wooden building that was painted an eye-popping, brighter-than-bright, shade of deep purple. An intricately carved fish dangled above the front door holding a sign that flapped in the wind. It read,

Dr. Fanny Sunshine Trout, Veterinarian
Fins, Feathers, Whiskers and Paws Welcome

Inside, an old Bobby Darin song was playing... "Somewhere, across the sea..." As his father carried the dog, Sam used his wheelchair to hold the door open to the office. And what an office it was!

"Uh-oh," Sam said under his breath. *This is very strange,* he thought. The walls of the reception area had been painted to look like the view from inside a fish tank!

Huh?

Imagine that you were a fish swimming in an aquarium surrounded by other fish, green plants and those funny little plastic things that people put in fish tanks. Now imagine that what the fish sees when people put their faces on the glass and smile or make faces at the fish. Okay? That's what's painted on Dr. Trout's walls. It's a fish's view of the world from inside a fish tank looking out at people like us.

"Oh, oh, oh, let me get the stretcher," said a young man with orange and grape hair, spiked straight up from the middle of his head, with fish scales tattooed around his neck. He jumped up from his seat at the receptionist desk and produced a stretcher in a snap. Then he ever so gently took Daring from Mr. Harris and placed her on the stretcher.

His nametag said **Grouper Finn, Assistant to Dr. Trout.**

With a closer look at Daring's condition, Grouper Finn pressed a button on his desk to summon the veterinarian.

Dr. Fanny Sunshine Trout rushed into the waiting room. She was tall and thin and wore eyeglasses with porpoise shaped frames. Fish hook earrings dangled from her ears. As she examined Daring, her lips puckered tighter than the freshest mackerel. "Oh, oh, oh, my, my, my, tish, tish, tish," she said, shaking her head.

"Three tishes?" Grouper Finn frowned. He knew that when the vet says three tishes it was very, very, very bad.

"I'm afraid so," she replied as she examined the poor dog, feeling every bone, running her fingers over its damaged body.

When she finished, Trout folded her slender body like a pretzel, knees to chin, until she was face-to-face with Sam.

"Your dog's hurt very, very, very bad, honey and I'm not sure there's anything I can do," she said, with so much compassion that her voice cracked. She sounded as if she would break into tears. Sam looked into her eyes, which seemed to swim behind her thick lenses. His thoughts raced through his mind as he struggled for what to say next.

"It's not our dog," Mr. Harris corrected her, breaking the silence. He reached over to comfort his son, placing a hand on his shoulder. Sam shrugged it away; shook his head vigorously.

"DAD!" Sam pleaded. He had a feeling that was so strong he could almost touch it. "I was hurt real bad in an accident and *I* lived. Give the dog a chance!"

"Sam, this isn't our dog, operations cost a lot of money." Mr. Harris turned to the vet. "I- I'm not working right now," his father stuttered, a little embarrassed in front of the vet.

A huge sob escaped from Sam's throat. "So we should just leave it to die?" Sam spun around and tugged on the vet's sleeve. "Please help her, Dr. Trout," he pleaded, "the dog's a fighter – I just know it."

Dr. Trout peered at Sam over the top of her glasses which had now slid down to the tip of her nose.

He reminds me of myself when I was a kid and found that injured cat in our back yard, she thought. She had nursed the cat back to health and had loved the cat so much she took him off to college with her.

In a swish, her mind was made up. Dr. Trout slid her glasses back in place and unfolded her body to her impressive height. "Here's the deal. If I operate for free will you promise to come by and visit her every day?" Sam shook his head vigorously as she continued. "It helps animals heal faster when they know there's someone who cares about them."

Sam's heart soared! "I promise!" Sam blurted, wiping his nose on his sleeve. Sam's determination surprised his father. He hadn't shown such strong interest in anything since the accident.

"We'll do our best, won't we, Sam?" Mr. Harris mumbled, wondering what he had just gotten himself into.

"Okey dokey artichokey," Trout said, signaling Grouper to wheel Daring into the operating room. "It's going to take hours. Go on home and I'll call you when I'm done."

Sam shook his head. "No way, we're staying right here."

"Come on, Sam. I have a lot of things to do at home and we haven't had lunch yet," Mr. Harris coaxed.

"Then leave me here and you go eat." Sam folded his arms across his chest. Believe it, he wasn't going to budge.

Mr. Harris sighed, shrugged and settled into a chair next to Sam.

To take his mind off the possible problems that they might encounter when the dog's owners came forward, he roamed through a stack of old *National Geographic* magazines until he found one that featured advances made in the field of robotics – a subject that he knew a great deal about.

cᴖ

After Grouper placed Daring on the operating table, he darted around the room to prepare for surgery. He set up sterile trays of instruments and went through a mental checklist to be sure everything needed would be close at hand. Once anesthesia was readied, Grouper and Trout scrubbed their hands, all the way up to their elbows while they both uttered "tish, tish, tish," over and over. Finally ready, they slipped into sterile gowns and gloves and got to work.

In the reception area, Sam and his dad discovered that they were not alone. Dr. Trout's pets were there to keep them company. Gil and Phil, a pair of cross-eyed Siamese cats, yowled nonstop as they rubbed against Sam's leg. Mackerel, an aging bulldog, lay wheezing at the door. Shifty, a colorful parrot, whose shorter leg caused him to stand lopsided on his perch, talked and sang in voices ranging from Rhianna to Elvis.

"Dad, will you get my video camera from the car?" Sam asked.

In a jiffy, Mr. Harris returned with the camera and handed it to Sam.

"These cats will look great in my video," Sam said, spinning around in his wheelchair, shooting from different angles, zooming in on the cats.

In the operating room, Trout cranked up an old Bee Gees tune to listen to as she operated. To relieve the tension, she executed a few cool disco steps as she moved around the operating table. "*More than a woman...*" she sang as her skilled fingers poked and pulled, molded and shaped. Grouper stood behind Daring's head, one hand on the mask covering Daring's nose and mouth, the other constantly checking Daring's vital signs.

"Hang in there, little girl," Grouper urged in his echo-like voice.

Daring's right rear leg kept flopping backwards. "Tish, tish, tish, this is a problem," Trout worried. Finally, after many attempts, Trout succeeded in getting it to stay put. Working feverishly, she stopped only to caress the unconscious dog and whisper encouragement in her ear. "Wish upon a star, little one – wish, wish, wish!"

The next track to play was Elvis Presley. Trout sang along, a little off-key, but with lots of enthusiasm, "*I Want You, I Need You, I Love You...*"

Hearing the singing coming from the operating room, Sam and his dad looked quizzically at each other.

"What is going on?" Sam asked nervously. Then Shifty joined in while swinging madly from his cage ... "*with all my heart"*... At Mr. Harris' feet, Mackerel snorted and snored, oblivious to the world.

Suddenly, Sam had his doubts." It's kind of weird here, Dad, do you think she knows what she's doing?" He'd never encountered singing in a medical office before. And he'd been in a lot of them.

Mr. Harris just smiled. "I think that dog just got lucky," he answered. Then he closed his eyes, leaned his head against the wall and called up the memory of his dear wife. *Oh, Louise – I wish you were here, my sweetheart. This is the first time our son has been excited about ANYTHING in such a long time. The problem is – if the owner claims the dog, Sam's heart will be broken all over again.*

Sam speed-dialed Lily. "Wait until you hear what happened today," he exclaimed. Sam told Lily the whole story – about finding the dog, the operation and the strange room he was waiting in. "Plus, I've got some great cat footage for our video," he announced, "I'll text you when I get home."

11
Wish Upon A Star

~

Under heavy anesthesia, Daring floated to the land of happy dreams. *Look at me, perfectly groomed, shiny and sparkly-eyed, eating real dog food from a clean dish. Oh look, I have a real ball that a boy is tossing nicely to me, instead of Cade's stinky shoe, that he throws so hard at me that my teeth wiggle. And best of all, I sleep on a nice thick bed, inside the house, instead of out in the cold, like he makes me when he says I'm bad. What's this? No more sneezing? I can TRACK – I can find lost people, catch bad guys ...* Daring dreamed of a bloodhound's life, for real. Even though she was sedated, the poor dog sighed heavily. This was just a wish, a dream that could never come true and she knew it.

As the hours ticked by, Dr. Fanny Sunshine Trout continued to work on the dog. Sam grew fidgety in his wheelchair. He began rolling himself around the room until he made his father dizzy. Meanwhile, Gil and Phil circled Shifty's cage, arching their backs, rolling their tails from side to side. Having had enough, Shifty began to meow, startling the stalking Siamese. Loving the action, Sam was grateful to have his video camera. As the animals carried on, Sam laughed so hard he could barely hold still his camera.

When he finally stopped shooting, Sam's stomach began to growl.

"Hungry, son?" Mr. Harris asked. They'd missed lunch and now it was almost time for dinner.

"How about we grab a sandwich, Sam? We won't take long and we can bring it back here if you like."

Sam wasn't having any of it. There was no way he would leave until the vet finished her surgery. "You go, Dad. I'll be fine if you bring me a tuna sandwich, just don't forget the chips."

"Back in a flash," Mr. Harris said as he bounded out the door.

Sam rolled his chair to the window and watched his dad drive away. *Hmmm, there's a weird feeling in this room*, Sam realized. He couldn't explain it. It just felt odd. As if on cue, Mackerel snorted, the cats' heads spun, and Shifty stopped warbling mid-swing. Something was definitely going on.

Whoosh! The waiting room door blew open. Even though it was cold outside, a soft, warm breeze flooded the room. Then it disappeared as quickly as it came. Sam shrugged his shoulders, pulled out his phone ready to make a call to Lily. Had Sam been looking in the direction of the operating room, he would have seen a flicker of golden dust dissolve through the door.

While Dr. Trout worked diligently to adjust Daring's legs, a shimmer of gold floated above the dog. It danced over and around Daring – ear-to-ear, foot-to-foot. Dr. Trout and Grouper were oblivious, concentrating only on saving the dog. They operated together like a well-rehearsed team. Grouper anticipated which instrument Trout would need before she asked for it, while keeping a keen eye on Daring. Maybe that was why Grouper missed the golden hue that filled the air like gossamer clouds of gold dust.

Suddenly, the shimmer of gold took on a shape as it hung suspended over Daring's head. It was a tiny figure, with the face of an eagle, its feathers made of gold and eyes made of rubies. With hummingbird-like beats of its golden wings, the figure hovered over Daring.

Although Daring was in a deep sleep, she looked bliss-ful, lost in a faraway dream. *I'm at a dog show and I – Daring Dog – am THE STAR OF THE SHOW!! Some of the finest dogs in the country are there; sleek athletes, fine prancers. But watch ME! I can JUMP—not just a little jump like on a chair, but high, higher than any dog has ever jumped. I am Awesome!* Daring's dream continues as the operation goes on. *Oh, wow –. I'm jumping over cars, trains, a store, and even a Ferris wheel!* But that's just the beginning. In her next dream, she was FLYING! Her ears were extended like wings, gravity pulled at her jowls, and her left front leg was tucked under her body while her right front leg was outstretched like a rudder. Her kinked tail now proved to be very useful as it helped her to steer. She flew over rooftops, swooping and soaring. Up, up and away! What's that below? Niagara Falls, the Statue of Liberty, Central Park. Yes—NEW YORK CITY!

While Daring dreamed on, Dr. Trout finished the opera-tion. It had taken over four hours. "Let's see how she did," she instructed Grouper, who removed the mask from her nose. For what seemed to be an eternity, Daring did not move. Then – her tail began to wag ever so slightly.

"That's the best I can do cutey-pie," Dr. Trout whispered to the groggy dog.

"She's a trouper," Grouper said. "A very, very, very brave girl!"

Daring sighed faintly when the vet bent to kiss the top of her head. Minutes later, Daring opened one eye. She raised her head, and looked around the strange room. When she heard Shifty singing, she realized that she wasn't dead. *I'm alive? Wow! I'm alive! Could it be that my luck has finally changed?* With a happy sigh, Daring dropped her head to her chest and fell back to sleep. Her body needed time to heal.

Dr. Trout entered the waiting room carrying Daring's worn collar and nametag. She looked exhausted. Her hair hung limp and the steam on her eyeglasses practically hid her eyes. Still, she managed an encouraging smile.

"Daring Dog's going to be fine," she said smiling warmly at Sam while handing him her collar. "Awesome!" he said, popping a wheelie. Mr. Harris hugged Sam tightly and then breathed a sigh of relief. He didn't dare think of the level of disappointment Sam would have felt had the dog died.

"Can I see her?" Sam begged.

"Sure, but not until tomorrow," Dr. Trout answered. "She's still pretty groggy and right now she needs to be absolutely quiet."

Sam understood. Although he wished with all his heart that he could just take a reassuring look at the dog, he knew that Dr. Trout was right.

"Go on home now and have your supper," she said as she opened her waiting room door. "Grouper is going to spend the night with her."

"What time can I come by tomorrow?" Sam asked as he pulled on his warm hat and zipped his jacket.

"How about you get here right after school."

"Okay, but can I call Grouper later to see how she's doing?"

Dr. Trout smiled down at the boy. "Sure, here's my card. Call before you go to sleep, okay?"

"Yeah, okay! Thanks Dr. Trout. I knew you could save her the minute I saw you."

Dr. Trout smiled softly as Mr. Harris shook her hand.

"I d-don't know how to th-th-thank you," he stuttered.

"She's not out of the woods yet," the vet cautioned. "Let's see what the morning will bring."

Sam and his father rode home silently, each lost in their own thoughts. One way or another, something huge had just happened in their lives. How huge, they had no idea.

12
Misty Harbor Lighthouse

~

Tired, but happy as clams, Sam and his father arrived home. Their house was small, but warm and comfortable. "Snug as bugs in a rug," Sam's mother used to say whenever they were lucky to be there as a family.

"Y'all are late," a stern voice drawled, as they entered the house.

"Sorry, Archie," Mr. Harris said to their housekeeper, "it's way past suppertime, so just heat up something simple while Sam starts his homework."

"We do not have SOMETHING SIMPLE on our menu. I am confused."

"Oh, sorry," Mr. Harris said, "What did you prepare for dinner?"

"Macaroni and meatballs is your dinner tonight."

"Yum," Sam yelled from his room.

"That's good, Archie. Thank you."

Archie whirred around to face Mr. Harris. "Dinner was ready at 5:30 p.m. Daylight Savings Time. It is 6:22 p.m. Please remember to call if y'all are late," Archie said still stern, but ever so polite.

Perhaps the most interesting thing about Archie was the way he was programmed to speak. Mr. Harris had created a very unusual voice for Archie. Instead of sounding like a robot, he sounded exactly like a former President of the United States – William Jefferson Clinton, who was originally from Arkansas and who spoke with a
L O N G, L I L T I N G, SOUTHERN D R A W L.

Mr. Harris had painstakingly created Archie's voice by taking clips from hundreds of the former president's television appearances. Sometimes, Archie sounded more like President Clinton than President Clinton did.

When they moved to Misty Harbor, Mr. Harris had to take the robot apart, because of its size, and then put it back together once they arrived. Once he had rebuilt Archie's body, Mr. Harris had spent the better part of a week programming Archie's GPS to load in maps of every square inch of the house, the lighthouse tower, the breakwater – rock by rock, every winding road and path in Misty Harbor – and the entire State of Maine! Mr. Harris had also added a bar codes reader so he could identify the food in the kitchen cabinets and refrigerator, and he affixed bar codes to the pots and pans, and all the appliances – so that with the GPS and his scanner, Archie could find everything!

Mr. Harris's preparation worked like a charm! Archie cooked delicious, nutritious meals, kept the house clean and neat, did the laundry, and answered the phone politely and efficiently. To make Archie appear a little more human, Mr. Harris sometimes wrapped a scarf around his neck, or on special occasions – a necktie. Archie wore a Red Sox shirt in baseball season, a New England Patriots jacket in the fall, and on days when it was so cold out that the biting wind whipped through cracks in the windows, Archie wore an old fisherman's sweater and matching hat. And he was always festive for the holidays.

At Halloween, the LED lights that surround the flat screen panel on Archie's chest flashed orange and black. For Thanksgiving, a turkey gobble made even a sullen Sam laugh his head off.

Archie had an elaborate hologram for Hanukah, featuring a menorah with candles that were lighted for each of eight days in the festival. The song "Dreidel, Dreidel, Dreidel' played each time a new candle was lit. When it was Kwanzaa, not only did Ziggy Marley sing, Archie was programmed to tap his arm to the Reggae beat. Now that Christmas was close, Archie had automatically downloaded selections of holiday music from iTunes. His favorite was "Rudolph the Red-Nosed Reindeer" which he had programmed to play ENDLESSLY.

Because the Harrises lived virtually on top of the ocean, weather was even more important than for those who lived on land. A howling gale wind could mean difficulty in walking across the breakwater to get to land. For that reason, the hologram on Archie's chest was programmed to deliver hourly weather reports.

When Sam and his dad had returned, the hologram read:

Cloudy skies, temperature 34 degrees Fahrenheit, wind East North East 20 – 25 miles per hour, chance of snow later in the day. BRRRR!!!

While Archie reheated dinner in the microwave, Sam wheeled himself through the great room that was really a combination dining and living room. Sam had loved coming to the house ever since he could remember. He could entertain himself just by feasting his eyes on the room's furnishings.

A colorful totem pole, over six feet tall, stood proudly in a corner of the room. Sam's mother had brought it back from Alaska several years earlier and Mr. Harris loved the piece so much he made certain to bring it when they moved to Misty Harbor.

Knowing that there were many symbols carved on totems, he had asked his wife why she had chosen this one, in particular. "Well, it wasn't easy," she had answered, "but once I thought about our family, I felt I made the right choice."

"Now you've got me interested," Mr. Harris had said when he'd studied the masterly carvings on the totem.

"The salmon symbolizes instinct, determination and persistence. I think that is a pretty fair description of you, Dave," Mrs. Harris had said with a smile. "The otter is a symbol of laughter, curiosity, grace and empathy, just like our little Sam."

Mr. Harris had agreed. "And what about you?" he asked.

"The Sea Turtle is Mother Earth – that was the easy one," Mrs. Harris had chuckled.

"And the eagle?" Mr. Harris asked, pointing to the top of the totem where a bald eagle topped the totem pole.

Mrs. Harris had grown quiet with a serious expression on her face. After a moment she had replied, "Ask me about the eagle another time, Dave, she had said, "I'll tell you about it, I promise."

Mr. Harris had been surprised by her reluctance. "Hmmm, that's not like you, Louise, have you forgotten?" he'd teased, pinching her chin tenderly.

A shadow had crossed her face. "Of course I haven't forgotten. For some reason, I just want to tell you another time, that's all."

Three pairs of well-worn snowshoes hung crisscrossed above the fireplace. One pair was almost fifty years old and had been used by Grampy Spencer right up until the time he had become ill. Various lengths and thicknesses of fishing rods and reels hung from hooks that were screwed into the thick beams that held up the roof. Bookshelves swayed under the weight of books and bric a brac, and paintings of old sailing ships lined the wall. Silver-framed photos of Sam and his father rested on the mantle, while other photographs were turned backwards toward the chimney. An assortment of rain gear, and winter wear were within easy reach of the front door.

A delicate curio cabinet stood in a prominent place in the living room. Along with the totem pole, it was one of the few things that Mr. Harris chose to bring to Misty Harbor. The cabinet was his wife's prized possession, made by Mr. Harris for their fifth wedding anniversary. He had spent weeks patiently rubbing the tiger maple wood until its golden hues took on a life of their own. Now, the cabinet stood as a reminder of how life used to be.

Next to the cabinet, a large cardboard box sat on the floor stuffed with carefully wrapped treasures that were once on display inside the cabinet.

After the accident, Sam had demanded that the cabinet be emptied. He'd told his father, "Mom will never see them again, so throw them away." Mr. Harris had ignored his son. He had hoped and prayed that some day Sam would change his mind and want to see his mother's treasures once again.

Since the accident, the hours Sam used to spend riding his bike and skateboarding, boogie-boarding in the ocean or playing soccer, were now spent in front of a row of computers, video equipment and a variety of other electronics, all designed and built by Mr. Harris – and mastered by Sam.

In fact, some of the software installed on Sam's computers was still in the experimental stage. "You'll get the bugs out for us," Mr. Harris had said as he explained what the software would allow Sam to do – or at least *try* to do. Sam had to admit that he was proud of the trust his father placed in him.

While waiting for Archie to set dinner on the table, Sam reached for his Smart Phone. "Call Lily," he said. He reached her voicemail. *She's probably practicing her tuba,* he thought, o*r maybe she was at rehearsal with the Misty Harbor marching band, or the school orchestra. Or maybe, she's out looking for Mrs. Grady's missing cat.*

"Dinner is served," Archie announced.

After Mr. Harris and Sam settled themselves at the table, Archie served the macaroni and meatballs.

"Perfectly prepared," Mr. Harris said cheerfully.

Sam chimed in. "Good JOB, Archie".

"Compliments accepted," the silver man said, bending at the knee in a tin man curtsy.

The evening's dessert was Mr. Harris' favorite – freshly baked apple pie topped with what looked like whipped cream. Mr. Harris plunged his fork into the yummy dessert, and then made a face.

"This is sour cream, Archie. Mistake."

"Mistake," repeated the robot. "Sorry," Archie apologized.

"Y'all were late. I hurried," Archie explained.

"No problem," Mr. Harris answered, although he had craved the whipped cream.

"Will that be all?" Archie asked.

"That will be all, Archie, thank you". Mr. Harris dabbed his chin with his napkin, while Archie cleared the table and began his kitchen chores.

After dinner, Sam did his homework on the computer while Mr. Harris worked in the boathouse. His winter project was building a graceful catboat so Sam could eventually learn to sail.

This was no ordinary catboat. Its body was shaped like an outstretched cat, the rudder formed like a tail, and the top of the mast was adorned with a carved cat's head and whiskers. Mr. Harris had designed a winch that would raise and lower the sails at the flick of a button, without Sam having to get up from his seat.

It was nearly ten that evening when the telephone rang. It was Dr. Trout offering her promised update on Daring's condition. "She's been awake, had a long drink of water and is asleep again," she reported.

"So she's really going to be okay?" Sam asked, his heart skipping a beat.

"Yes, yes, yes, she is going to be fine and Grouper is with her. Just be sure to dream something wonderful about her tonight when you go to bed."

"And nobody's come looking for her?" Sam asked, crossing his fingers.

"No, Sam," Dr. Trout said, "but I don't want to make promises I am not one hundred percent sure I can keep, but I have a funny feeling that no one will."

"When will we know?" Sam pressed on.

"It's a ten-day holding period, then, if no one claims her, she can be put out for adoption."

"So nine days from today, right?" Sam wondered if he could stand the suspense.

"Yes, right." The vet paused, she knew that Sam had his heart set on keeping this dog.

"Sam, just so you know," she continued. "In such a small town, word gets out pretty fast about a missing pet, especially a purebred bloodhound. Usually people call the police, the animal shelter and the local vets. I haven't received a call, so just be patient," she urged. "Let's hope what's best for Daring is best for all of us. Promise me you won't get your hopes up."

"Well, what's best for Daring is – *me!*"

Later, when his dad planted a goodnight kiss on the top of his head, Sam reached for him and kissed him back – something he hadn't done for a long time. Then he looked intently at his father.

"No matter what the chances are, Daring is going to make it!"

"I hope so, son," Mr. Harris said as he stroked Sam's unruly mop of hair.

"Really Dad, I know it in my heart," Sam said as he settled onto his pillows, "and if no one comes for her in nine more days, Daring is going to be mine!" Although Sam knew it was wrong to wish for – he hoped and prayed that Daring's owner was never found.

In a wink, Sam was asleep, floating in the land of *good* dreams – finally. His sleep was so deep that he wasn't aware of a breeze that had blown into his room, nor did he see the shimmer of gold dust that lingered over his bed. Although he was sleeping, Sam flicked his fingers over his cheek, thinking that he felt something there– a whisper of a touch – a *kiss* as light as a feather.

With his arms cradling his pillow, his down quilt pulled up to his chin, Sam smiled, lost in a dream about Daring. He was teaching her tricks, they were cuddling on his bed. She would be his most loyal friend. A new beginning.

13
Visiting Hours
~

Today is the longest school day ever! Sam moaned to himself. He was so excited to visit Daring, that not even a fart noise and finger pointing in his direction from Basil Pettibone could rattle him.

When Lily's mom said she could go along and meet Daring, Sam was thrilled. "Wait til you meet MY DOG!" he gushed on the short ride to the vet's office.

Dr. Fanny Sunshine Trout and Grouper Finn greeted them warmly when they arrived.

Dr. Trout wore earrings shaped like frogs, with lily pads dangling from silver chains. Her T-shirt had a large octopus on it with the message "Hug me". Dr. Trout might be the most unusual person Lily had ever seen up close. "This place is so cool," Lilly uttered, and then burst into a big smile, showing off her bright blue braces.

"Pleased to meet you," Lily said, like her mother had taught her.

"Woof," answered Dr. Trout, who beckoned them to follow her to the back of her clinic.

When they reached Daring's cage and got their first look at Daring since her operation, Sam and Lily, and even Mr. Harris, G A S P E D!!!

Lily covered her eyes. "She's all broken, Sam," she cried, "I'm scared to look at her."

Sam squinted his eyes, he could barely see the dog under all of the surgical dressings. In addition to her bandages. Daring wore a large crinkly collar so she wouldn't be able to lick or chew her wounds. A good amount of her fur had been shaved off.

"Wow! Sam turned to Dr. Trout. "Wow, wow, wow!"

The vet was confused. "Wow?" she asked, "what do you mean, I'm confused?"

Sam looked very serious. "Yeah, wow! She has more bandages than I had – and that was a lot!"

"Well, okay then, Dr. Trout smiled. "If you move closer, she will be able to see you – or at least smell you."

Lily peeked from between her fingers, then slowly reached out to touch the dog.

"She's beautiful!" Lily said, hesitating before reaching out to gently pat Daring's head.

In truth, Daring looked pretty awful. She was drooling faster than Grouper could wipe it up. Her eyes were glazed and filled with fear.

"You're going to be fine, Daring," Sam reassured her, stroking the top of Daring's head – the only place where she was not bandaged.

"I forgot what Sam said, what kind of a dog is she?" Lily asked Dr. Trout.

"Daring is a bloodhound, one of the smartest dogs in the universe," Dr. Trout replied.

Lily thought for a moment. "Why do they call her a bloodhound? Does she drink blood or something?" Lily stuck out her tongue at the thought.

"You're gross, Lily," Sam said. "Last night I looked up bloodhounds online," he explained, "they can follow the scent of blood for miles, that's why the cops use them when people get lost."

"Right-o, Sam," said Dr. Trout. She patted Daring's head and then knelt next to the children. "See all these folds in her skin on her face?"

Sam and Lily nodded.

"And see how deep set her eyes are in her head?"

They nodded again.

"Those are the marks of a champion," the vet said, running her hand along what remained of Daring's fur. "Well, all except for her ears, they're a little long, but who cares? Once she gets some good food in her and has exercise and fresh air, she'll be a humdinger!"

"A champion?" Lily exclaimed.

"I don't care if she gets a booby prize. I want to keep her," Sam was adamant.

Dr. Trout frowned, she knew the law. No matter what, Daring belonged to her owner if she was claimed within a certain amount of time. They had eight more days to go. The last thing she wanted was to disappoint this boy who had evidently been through so much.

"She must have an owner, Sam, a dog like this with champion markings. I just don't understand why she is so skinny. In fact, I plan to have a serious talk with the owners when they come to get her."

Sam grew quiet. He had blocked any thought of not being able to keep the dog.

"How will the owners know where she is?" Lily asked with an eye on Sam who was furiously biting his lip.

"Usually we'll get a call from the pound, or from the police," the vet explained, "I'm surprised I haven't heard from them yet."

"What happens if no one calls?" Sam asked hopefully.

"After ten days the dog can be adopted." Dr. Trout smiled softly and rested her hand on Sam's shoulder. "Yes, Sam, there are eight more days to go.

"Can a kid adopt a dog?" he asked tentatively.

"Actually, your dad would have to sign for it and take full responsibility," she explained, "but you're getting ahead of yourself, Sam. Like I told you last night, we have to wait and see."

Sam shook his head, trying to appear cooperative and understanding, but then he blurted, "I hope no one comes for her so I can take her home." Sam was determined that Daring was going to be his.

On the ride home, Sam felt a warm breeze tickle the back of his neck. Thinking it was Lily playing a joke, he reached behind his head to grab her hand, surprised that it wasn't there. Lily was right beside him with both hands in her lap. *Hmm. A warm wind is blowing off the freezing, cold ocean,* he thought. *Strange.*

14
Welcome To The Family

~

It felt like forever as the days dragged on. Sam had grown short-tempered with his father, been testy with his teacher and especially hostile to his physical therapist. The waiting was driving him crazy. Only Lily seemed to understand that Sam needed to be eased up on.

"Just go along as if everything is normal," Lily's mother had told her. "If you want to go see Daring with Sam tomorrow, you can skip your chores."

Lily ran to her Smart Phone to text Sam.

LC. Cn I vzit Daring w/u?

Sam didn't hesitate. He liked having Lily interested in Daring.

SH: k

LC: Onr shO up yet?

SH: N!

LC: kewl

SH: 3 mo days & she's myn

LC: yay

When the weekend arrived, Lily showed up at Sam's to work on the video they were making for their school project.

"How come you put up that clip on YouTube?" Lily asked, "we're not even finished with it yet."

"It's just a tease, besides, Mrs. Grady is going nuts," Sam answered, "she calls all the time and talks to Archie."

Lily thought for a moment and ran her tongue over her blue braces. "Ok, I just hope that cat isn't frozen to death. It's really cold outside."

"We'll find it, I just have a feeling," Sam smiled and turned to his computer.

"Tell me how you like this, I put some special effects on the title," Sam said as his fingers swept over the keyboard.

Lily watched as letters animated up from a Sherlock Holmes pipe.

THE SEARCH FOR PRINCE CHARMING
starring Lily Cohen
directed by Sam Harris

"Like it?" he asked Lily.

"Oh yeah! And we're going to add music, too – right?" Lily asked, excited when she saw her name on the screen.

"Sure, just as soon as we finish the edit. You're the musician, so *you* pick the music. Okay?"

"Okay," she answered, grinning at the thought of scoring music to a video.

They got to work by scanning the footage they'd collected. There were dozens of different Siamese cats hiding in a variety of different places that you might never think of – places like a man's boot, a bureau drawer, under a pillow, and in a pile of dirty laundry. Unfortunately, Prince Charming wasn't among them.

The following Monday, Day Nine of the waiting period, Lily's mother volunteered to pick up Sam and Lily after school so they could visit Daring at Dr Trout's office. They would be able to spend the good part of an hour talking to the dog, petting her head and just being near her cage. Mr. Harris was grateful for her offer.

As they were saying goodbye to Daring, Dr. Trout joined them in front of her cage. "Daring's taking a little more time to recover than I would have thought, probably because she's so skinny," she said as she ran her hands over Daring's ribs. "I don't think she ever had much to eat." The vet pursed her lips and shook her head disapprovingly, "Tish, tish, tish".

"Has anyone called about her yet?" Sam asked, barely able to get the words out of his mouth.

Dr. Trout took a deep breath, smiled broadly, and then turned to Grouper. "Has anyone called about Daring?"

"Nope," he said, struggling to keep from grinning.

Sam exhaled and uncrossed his fingers.

Dr. Trout looked at Lily and then Sam. Then, she bent down like a pretzel to give Sam a giant hug.

"I just got off the phone with your dad," she said quietly. Sam held his breath as she continued.

"Since it's after 2 p.m., technically, we've just begun Day Ten of the waiting period, so it looks like you've got yourself a bloodhound!"

Sam felt his heart swell in his chest and then for some unknown reason he started to weep. He was overcome with joy. Lily jumped up and down and cheered, "AWESOME! That's so AWESOME, AWESOME, AWESOME!"

"You're coming home with me, girl!" Sam said as he carefully put his arms around her neck and tried to nuzzle her nose. He held out his Smart Phone, hit Instagram, and took a "selfie" of himself with his dog. *His dog!*

A second later, Daring raised her head, then sneezed, hurling a blob of snot that landed squarely on Sam's cheek.

"Gross!" Lily cringed.

"Not for me," Sam said, taking a tissue from Dr. Trout, "and don't you ever call MY DOG gross again!"

Dr. Trout had prepared a file folder filled with notes about Daring, the care she will need, the food she can eat, when to walk her – everything Sam needed to know to give Daring a proper home.

"Just let me keep her one more night, then you can pick her up and take her home," Dr. Trout said.

"Promise?" Sam asked.

"You can count on it," Dr. Trout promised. "Daring Dog belongs to you, Samuel Harris. I will have official paperwork for your dad to sign when you pick her up tomorrow."

"I can't believe it," Sam exclaimed. "This is the best!"

"Now go on home and get working on this list of things she'll need. She's your responsibility now," Dr. Trout said as she walked them to the door.

On the ride home, Sam and Lily talked a mile a minute, planning where he'd place Daring's bed, checking the folder to see what kind of food she'd eat, and how soon it would be before he could teach her some tricks.

They were so excited they barely noticed Basil, who was walking with two of his bully buddies. The boys smirked and hooted when they noticed Sam and Lily drive by.

In less than a minute Sam received a text alert. It was Basil.

BP: U R a 3: o)

Sam showed the text to Lily. "What does *this* mean? Is it some Misty Harbor thing?"

"It means *you are a girl*. See the hair, eyes, nose and mouth?"

They both laughed at the absurdity.

And for once, Sam totally ignored the text. He had more important things on his mind.

"Thank you, thank you, thank you! This is so awesome," he said to his dad. And it almost was except…

15
Too Good To Be True
~

Later that night, Daring's short streak of good luck ran out. Drawn back to Misty Harbor by his desire for more goods to steal, Cade cruised around town deciding on his next victim.

Unfortunately, Cade came upon the office of Dr. Fanny Sunshine Trout. *BINGO,* he thought. He drove around back of the building, parked his truck, broke in, stole what he thought to be the most expensive of Dr. Trout's supplies, and was about to leave when he spied Daring recuperating in a cage.

"I'll be a monkey's uncle!" Cade laughed, "Look what the cat dragged in!" He squinted at the dog.

"You look pretty crappy, girl – but I can still sell a Royal Scent bloodhound!" He was so excited to find Daring that he dropped his cigarette on a stack of shredded newspaper as he reached for the door of her cage. The newspaper quickly burst into flames!

"Crap," he exclaimed. "Oh no, he moaned, "Man, oh man, this is a bad scene!"

Cade grabbed a nearby blanket and tried to beat out the flames, but the fire spread faster than he could put it out.

Suddenly, the sprinkler system began to spray and the fire alarm in the security system blared a warning.

I'm out of here, he thought as he ran out the door.

Leaving Daring and his loot behind, Cade raced from the building in a panic, jumped into his truck and drove off.

"NO!" screamed Dr. Trout.

The moment she heard the alarm and smelled smoke from her apartment above the clinic, she jumped out of bed, ran downstairs and grabbed Gil and Phil. She put Shifty on her shoulder and shooed Mackerel out the door. The fire truck arrived as she frantically shoved her pets into the cab of her truck. Without a moment to spare, Dr. Trout ran back for Daring, but the smoke was too thick and a fireman stopped her from entering the building.

"There's a dog in a cage in there," she screamed, "please, I have to go in." Dr. Trout was frantic, walking in a circle, chanting "Tish, tish, tish – tish, tish, TISH!"

"Don't worry, we'll find it," the firefighter assured her.

"Be gentle," Dr. Trout pleaded, "she just had surgery!"

Overcome by smoke, Daring drifted into a stupor. In her hazy mind, Daring thought she saw a tiny golden eagle. The eagle flapped her wings creating a cool breeze over Daring's body. From somewhere beyond the eagle, Daring heard chanting. Daring's eyelids fluttered open, she raised her head and a blast of fresh air filled her lungs.

"Easy does it," the firefighter said while cradling her carefully in his arms.

"Thank GOD!" Dr. Trout exclaimed when she saw that Daring's eyes were open and she appeared to be okay. With the help of the firefighter, Dr. Trout quickly examined the dog, and then lowered her onto the back of her truck. Then she covered Daring with some blankets that she kept in the cab of her truck, tucked her in tightly and said a silent prayer of thanks.

Sam was right, Dr. Trout thought. Daring Dog was a survivor!

Relieved that no one has been injured, but stunned at the loss of her clinic and apartment, Dr. Trout sat in her truck weeping and tishing. How could such a senseless thing happen? With the clinic in ruin, she must find homes for herself and the animals. *At least I know where I can bring Daring,* she realized. After taking a few deep breaths and calming herself as best she could, she drove off toward the lighthouse.

Dr. Fanny Sunshine Trout was a sorry sight when she knocked on the Harrises' door, her eyeglasses fogged, her clothing covered with soot and ashes.

Sam and his father were at the door the moment they heard her truck rumbling down the breakwater road. Sam had seen the fire alert come through on his browser and was trembling with fear.

"She's dead, isn't she?" Sam asked, close to hysteria.

Dr. Trout smiled for the first time since the fire had begun. "No, Sam, she's in the back of the truck. You can see for yourself."

Sam wheeled himself to the truck and laughed and sobbed joyful tears when he saw Daring lying under the blankets, seemingly without a care in the world. She was fast asleep.

Dr. Trout was freezing as she stood by her truck. It was then that she realized she was wearing only her flannel pajamas under her ski parka.

"Let's get Daring in the house," she said as she climbed into the back of her truck and passed Daring to Mr. Harris.

"We haven't got her bed yet, but I can make one in a jiffy," Mr. Harris said. "Let's get Daring settled fast," Dr. Trout said nearly out of breath.

"I've got a piece of foam rubber and an old bedspread in the boathouse," Mr. Harris remembered. He returned in less than a minute with the makings of a wonderful bed for Daring that they set up in a corner of Sam's bedroom. Sam was overjoyed!

Once they had Daring settled, Dr. Trout headed back to her truck.

"Come back inside and warm up," Mr. Harris insisted.

"Thanks, but I have to leave the truck engine running. My animals need to stay warm," she explained.

"No problem, please come in and tell us what happened," Mr. Harris insisted.

After two cups of cocoa and warming herself in front of the fireplace, she finally stopped shivering and was able to tell Sam and his dad the little that she knew about how and when the fire started.

"How can we help?" Mr. Harris asked.

"Oh … well, well, well …" Dr. Trout got up her nerve. Under ordinary circumstances she was very independent. But this was a real emergency and she knew that she had no choice but to ask for help.

"I know I barely know you and I have no right to ask, but could my pets stay with you for just a little while?" she began. "My mom lives in a tiny apartment and the landlord doesn't allow pets."

"All of them?" Mr. Harris asked incredulously. He was busy working on a new computer program for Archie; the house was small and he wanted to finish the boat. Pets are messy. Mr. Harris could think of a million reasons why he didn't want to have her animals stay with them, but when he saw how pathetic Dr. Trout looked, he just sighed, and sighed, and sighed.

"I can take Mackerel to Grouper's house," she offered. "He has five dogs already but Mackerel's been there before and they all get along." Dr. Trout's lips often puckered in and out whenever she was nervous. They were moving wildly at the moment.

"Dad!" Sam shouted. His father always took so long to make a decision, likes to think things through, to consider all of the possibilities. Yet, Dr. Trout's simple request seemed like a no-brainer.

Picking up on his son's cue, Mr. Harris shook his head to unscramble his brains. "O-o-kay, I mean, of course we'll help you out. In fact, we'll keep Mackerel here, too. It would probably be best for them to keep them together," Mr. Harris reasoned, "After what you've done for Daring, it's the least we can do."

Sam wheeled himself to his father and gave him a tight squeeze.

"Thanks," said Sam, smiling from ear to ear.

Dr. Trout hugged Mr. Harris too! She was so grateful that she began flapping her arms as if they were wings.

Dr. Trout threw her jacket over Shifty's cage to protect him from the cold wind as she carried him into the house. She found a nice spot for him in the living room, near enough to a window but far enough away from a draft.

Gil and Phil were carried in next, hissing and spitting, showing their fangs and flicking their tails. Like all cats, they promptly disappeared until they could size up their situation and decide when it would safe to come out. "I can pick up a litter box at the grocery store," Dr. Trout offered.

Mr. Harris turned Archie's switch into "awake" mode. "I'm going to have to re-program Archie's GPS. It will only take a minute or two."

"What are those?" Archie asked, pointing to the cats.

Dr. Trout was taken aback for a moment.

"This is Archie, Dr. Trout. He takes care of us, cooks, cleans – what-not," Mr. Harris explained.

"What are those?" Shifty parroted. Archie's head rotated. Indeed, what was *that?*

Mackerel was the last of Dr. Trout's precious pets to be brought in. When he saw Archie, he stood frozen to the spot.

"Dello hawg," Archie drawled. As clever as Mr. Harris was, Archie had a glitch. Every once in awhile, Archie mixed up the first letters of words. This was one of those times. Sam wheeled himself to Archie and pressed a black reset button on the robot. It was located where his belly button would have been if he were a human.

"Hello dawg," Archie said correctly.

"Clever," observed Dr. Trout, impressed that the Harrises had a robot.

"Yes, well he needs some fine tuning," Mr. Harris explained.

"He puts sour cream on apple pie – things like that," Sam added.

Flamingo pink and acid green lights flashed from Archie's chest. His head tilted side to side. Mackerel wagged his stubby tail, wheezed and snorted, until he found a warm spot in front of the fireplace to stretch out and go to sleep.

"I'll bring food and supplies for them tomorrow," Dr. Trout reassured Mr. Harris, while shaking his hand and then giving Sam a hug. "I don't know how to thank you," she said, her eyes brimming with tears, "it won't be for long,

I promise. I'll take them back just as soon as I can set up shop."

"T-take as long as you n-need," Mr. Harris mumbled, a little nervous about the menagerie that was now living in his house.

"I'm very, very, very grateful," she said, wiping away a tear. Finally, Dr. Trout rumbled off down the breakwater and continued into Misty Harbor.

After checking on his sleeping dog, Sam texted Lily:

SH: She's om

LC: OMG. Saw d fire on tv. teL me evrtng

SH: aL pets k. cum hEr aftR skul

LC: k

SH: U won't BlEv how kewl my dad iz. G'nite

It was very late before Sam was able to get to bed. Although a terrible tragedy had been avoided, the fear that Sam felt when he saw the fire on his computer had deeply upset him. Still, nothing could match the comforting sight of Daring, on her bed just an arm's length away from his own.

"Have a good sleep," he told Daring, patting her head, "you're home now!"

Although he was asleep the minute his head hit the pillow, it took little time for Sam's nightmares to return:

It's all mixed up. I'm freezing cold but the man putting the harness around me is a FIREMAN. Why is he here? Where is the fire? I hear the dog barking. Up, up, up. No it doesn't hurt. I don't feel ANYTHING!

Sam tossed and turned, heaving his quilts, muttering and gasping as he tried to sort out the images in his dream that clearly didn't go together. As he struggled in his sleep, Daring woke up. After watching Sam's struggle, somehow, Daring was able to hoist herself up. With her last bit of strength, Daring found Sam's hand dangling from the side of his mattress, and gave it a good, bloodhound lick. This time, it was not only his father's gentle touch that awakened him, it was the loving touch of a dog – his dog. Daring Dog.

16
Home Sweet Home
~

The next day Shifty sat silently pecking his feathers, refusing to eat. Instead, he moaned and groaned, sounding like an old man. "I'm dying, I'm dying," he croaked.

"Archie, please bring me a pretzel," Sam said.

Archie's computer brought forth the bar code for pretzels and directed him to the proper kitchen cabinet.

"Here you go, buddy," Sam said, as he passed the treat to the bird. After one bite, the parrot spit it out. Undaunted, Sam slid a piece of bacon into the cage. "Bet you can't resist that," Sam teased.

Shifty took the crispy meat into his beak and spit it out.

Archie stood in front of Sam with a plate of sliced oranges. "Y'all have to have your vitamin C," he drawled. As Archie passed the plate to Sam, Shifty slipped his claw out of the cage and snatched a piece. He began beaking away at the orange, taking small bits and swallowing them.

"It appears that his hunger strike is over," Mr. Harris said when Shifty greedily accepted another slice from Sam. Meanwhile, Archie's computer had searched for favorite treats for parrots. As soon as the bar code registered, Archie was busy in the kitchen preparing treats for the bird.

"Y'all will like this," Archie said as he brought a slice of green pepper to Sam. "The African gray parrot likes green pepper."

"Wow, Archie! How did you know what kind of parrot he is?"

"To identify the bird, my iCamera photographed it, then went for recognition in its files. The bird is an African Grey Parrot – its scientific name is *Psittacus erithacus*. The African Grey Parrot is found in the rainforests of West and Central Africa. Experts regard it as one of the most intelligent birds in the world. They feed primarily on palm nuts, seeds, fruits, and leafy matter, but have also been observed eating snails."

"Snails?" Sam questioned.

"Snails, according to Wikipedia." Archie returned to the kitchen to do the dishes.

The minute Shifty saw the green pepper, he grabbed it and clucked his pleasure. After a few more slices of orange, green pepper and spinach, Sam had Shifty eating out of his hand.

Later that morning, Shifty was in rare form! "*Blue, blue, blue suede shoes,*" Shifty sang in Elvis Presley's voice, while rocking back and forth in his cage. He finished the song, then talked a blue streak, chirping, "*You've got mail*" often enough to get on Sam's nerves. "Okay Shifty, time out," Sam pleaded. "I have to work on my video and I can't hear the audio."

Gil and Phil sprung into action. They circled Shifty's cage, stalking and swatting, until Shifty barked back, freaking them out, even though he'd done this dozens of times.

"Oh, you guys are good!" Sam exclaimed as he caught the action on his video camera. He e-mailed a clip to Lily.

Meanwhile, Daring had perked up considerably after eating the boiled hamburger and rice breakfast Archie had cooked for her. Something in her memory reminded her of the smell of cooked hamburger. *The Masons,* she thought.

Archie poured fresh, cool water into a shiny silver bowl. *This tastes wonderful,* Daring thought as she lapped the bowl dry.

Still, Daring didn't completely trust the Harrises' kindness. The bandages confused her, as did the pain she felt when she moved. She'd been mistreated and abused her whole adult life, so it was understandable that when Sam wheeled himself toward her, she cowered, waiting for the slap that she'd come to expect. When it didn't come, she looked up at Sam with her big brown eyes and allowed herself to sigh when he patted her gently and praised her.

"Good dog, Daring," Sam reassured her. Still, she trembled at the touch of a human.

"Don't be scared, girl," Sam petted her tenderly, "I know what it's like to wake up in a strange place, all bandaged and hurt." Daring sighed, her trembling stopped. *The boy's touch feels good,* she thought. *His voice is soft and kind. If only I could stay here and never see Cade again.*

As the days went by, Daring grew stronger. A week after the fire, she was able to sit up without yelping in pain.

"Good dog," Sam praised her, "just take it slow, Daring, one day at a time." Sam had learned a lot from his own therapy and now he was able to use his experience to help his dog.

A week later, a Misty Harbor miracle occurred. With Sam's gentle encouragement, Daring was able to walk to the door!

"Good girl!" Sam said proudly.

"Let's go, girl!" Mr. Harris put a leash on her to walk her outside so she could relieve herself. When she returned, Sam praised her again, and then sneaked a tiny piece of pizza to her. It was her first taste of freshly cooked, still-warm cheese and she loved it.

"Pizza is not a dawg food," Archie said.

Ignoring him, Sam said, "Have some more, girl," He pulled a piece of melted cheese from his slice and held it close to her mouth. Greedily, Daring lapped it off and wow – she could wag her crooked tail!

When she went back to her bed, Sam patted her head and scratched behind her ears. A new feeling came over Daring. *Strange,* she thought, *but nice.* Later, when Sam slipped one of his extra bed pillows under her head, Daring's heart melted. Quite suddenly, she realized that she was madly in love with Sam. Daring realized, *I'm not sad anymore!*

17
All You Need Is Love

~

Once she was able to walk more easily, Daring followed Sam everywhere, content to sit next to his wheelchair, or snore at the foot of his bed. When Sam went to school, Daring sat obediently in the house waiting for his return. A few minutes before the school bus was due to arrive, Mr. Harris would walk Daring to the end of the breakwater, where she would sit patiently, until whopping her tail wildly when she heard the school bus coming down the road. When Sam tied a bandana around her neck to catch some of her drool, Daring nearly drowned him with loving laps and big sneezes. She even tried to heek out a love song. Although she couldn't really sing, her high-and low-pitched whine sounded as tender and loving as a dog's voice could be.

Even better than her heeking, Daring had begun to smile – a crooked smile that only a bloodhound can produce – slobber and all, but it was a smile, nonetheless. Content to be near Sam and to feel the love he had for her, Daring Dog's dreams – and you can bet dogs certainly do dream – had come true.

Mr. Harris knew that Daring had begun to fill a place in Sam's heart that had been empty since the accident. In just a few days, there had been a big change in Sam. He ate his vegetables without encouragement and whistled happily while doing his chores. In fact, Sam hadn't complained once about anything, except – Mr. Harris wouldn't stop trying to yodel.

"Dad, stop, PLEASE!"

Sam wasn't trying to be mean. The truth was that instead of a melodious, catchy, somewhat fascinating yodel, Mr. Harris could only make weird cackling sounds that came from the back of his throat. It sounded like someone was strumming his vocal chords with a fork. And it made the hair on the back of Sam's neck stand up straight.

Worse still, Shifty had begun to croadel (that terrible combination of croaking and yodeling)! And if that wasn't enough, when the yodeling and croadeling started, Gil and Phil yowled at the top of their lungs. Not to be outdone, Shifty injected some meows into his croadeling. It was enough to drive a sane person mad. It was so excruciating that Sam put his fingers in his ears and yelled, "Stop, stop!" When there was no sign that it would end soon, Sam would slip on his headphones and crank up the volume. It was tough for Daring, too. The dog dashed around the room trying to find something to stick her head under.

The little house was beginning to have a life of it's own. There was a new energy, a feeling of excitement, a bulging, happy, a bit out-of-control household that was beginning to feel like a home.

18
Stand Up and Be Counted

~

With all the chaos going on at home with a hastily repro-grammed Archie, and Mr. Harris tending to Dr. Trout's mini zoo, Sam was actually eager to be going off to school. On this particular day, it was freezing cold out, with a frosty North wind blowing straight down from Canada. To keep warm, Sam wore his most prized possession, a red, black and white woolen hat with earflaps that fastened under his chin. The top of the hat was embroidered in an Inuit design – a big frog, which meant something special to the Inuit and to Sam, but nothing to Basil and his buddy, Fingers. The hat was so precious to Sam that he sometimes slept with it.

After the bus driver and Mr. Harris settled Sam in his seat, Fingers flicked something at him, hitting him in the head.

"Real smooth, Fingers," Sam said, disgusted. Lily got up from her seat and moved next to Sam.

"Isn't that a girl's hat?" Basil taunted. "My aunt has one just like it."

"Drop it, you dweeb," Lily warned. Other kids slid down in their seats, not wanting to be on the receiving end of whatever Basil, Fingers and now, the other Crabs, were flicking at Sam.

Although he could feel a fury growing inside, Sam stayed calm. "Forget it, Lily," Sam said adjusting his hat, "you can't expect someone like Basil to know what he's talking about." Sam was right, but the problem was that Basil had a group of friends who sided with him.

"They're always jerks when someone new comes to school, but that doesn't make it right," Lily whispered.

"CUT IT OUT BACK THERE!" the bus driver warned. For the moment, Basil and his buddies settled down.

During lunch, Lily found Basil, Fingers and their friends in the cafeteria. She marched up to them, ready to give them a piece of her mind.

"That was Sam's *mother's* hat. You shouldn't say those things to him," she scolded.

"What's he, your boyfriend?" Basil laughed, curling his lips and making a nasty face.

"No, stupid, he's my *friend,* who just happens to be a boy."

The tone of her voice really irked Basil. He tried to rattle Lily by making a rude noise, but Lily ignored him. Then to get her attention, Basil ripped a piece of blue paper from his notebook, pasted it over his teeth, and smiled at Lily.

"You are so pathetic," she said, then she turned to glare at Fingers.

"Everyone knows what happened to Sam and his mother," Lily said. Fingers pretended that he wasn't listening. To gross her out, he popped a pimple on his chin.

Unfazed and feeling brave, Lily continued. "None of us have ever done half the things that Sam did with his mother.

She was amazing, she wrote books about whales! And in the summer they went to Alaska and Greenland and …"

Fingers rolled his eyes. "Hey, we have enough snow here in the winter, thank you. Only a doofus would want to see more snow in the summer." Fingers slapped Basil on the back to make his point, except his timing was bad. Basil had a mouthful of macaroni and cheese that he spit on the table, grossing everyone out.

"*You're* the doofus, Fingers." Lily shook her head. "You just don't get it. Sam has ridden on a dogsled! He's seen polar bears and huge brown bears catching fish with their paws. And eagles, up close… and whales jumping all the way out of the water!"

"Duh!" was all Basil could manage, while Fingers started to jump up and down, blowing through his nose, pretending to be a whale.

Lily was exasperated. She couldn't believe how shallow these boys were. Still, she didn't give up "… and Sam has a robot in his house that cooks and does the laundry!"

"Whoopie! Where'd that get him? A wheelchair!" Basil shouted, getting the attention of the cafeteria monitor, who started to approach him.

Basil knew it was time to leave, but Lily blocked him. "Seriously, you should see the pictures in his house. Sam actually stood on a glacier and the ice is blue!" She was desperate to impress upon Basil and Fingers that Sam was a great kid to know. "He has pictures of polar bears that his mom took."

"Grrrr," Basil clawed his fingers and bared his teeth as he passed her.

"Of course, you're too much of an idiot to go to his house. Imagine if it was *your* mother, Basil."

Lily became so emotional that she began to sob. Although a tear slid down her cheek, she didn't back off. "Sam's mom is dead and he's never going to see her again, she said emotionally, "and all you can do is make fun of him."

That remark finally got to them. Basil, Fingers and all of the Crabs were quiet as they slinked out of the cafeteria. That was a first.

☙

On the bus ride home, the Crabs avoided looking at Lily. Surprisingly, no one picked on Sam, but the spell was broken when they got their first glimpse of Daring, who was waiting with Mr. Harris.

When the bus pulled to a stop, Daring bayed like a lovesick seal. Her crooked tail wagged and her drool flew in globs and strands.

"No way!" shouted Basil, pointing his finger at a stream of drool that had landed on the bus window next to his seat. The Crabs hooted and laughed, pointing at the dog.

"She's scary looking!" Fingers exclaimed, "she's almost bald!"

"Look at that goofy look on her face! Where'd you get her, Sam, at the dump?" Fingers laughed so hard that he clutched his stomach.

"They're just jealous," Sam consoled Daring, who knew they were making fun of her. She lowered her head as she walked next to Sam's wheelchair.

Hey, I've heard it before, no biggie, Daring thought. A strand of drool glistened brightly in the sunshine. Suddenly, Daring stopped, scratched for fleas, got up, and proceeded to slip on a patch of ice. When she got up, she sneezed and bounced higher than Sam's head.

Sam was astonished. "Did you see that, Dad?"

"See what?" Mr. Harris had been looking in the other direction and missed it.

"Daring jumped as high as my head!"

"Oh, that's nice, Sam." Mr. Harris was off in one of his scientific fogs again.

They stopped at the boathouse, where Sam watched for a few minutes as his father returned to work on Archie. Within seconds, Mr. Harris had a can of oil in one hand and a computer keyboard balanced on his lap.

"Guess we get our own snack," Sam said to Daring.

Sam rolled into the house with Daring at his side. He found a plate of cookies on the counter waiting for him. There were a few milk bones for Daring. "Thanks, Archie!" he called out the door.

"Y'all are welcome," Archie answered from the boathouse.

As Sam sat eating a cookie, he reached over to pat Daring's head.

"You're my buddy, Daring. It's just you and me... and Lily, of course." It was then that Sam realized how lonely he's been.

His text alarm sounded. Assuming it was Lily, he pulled his Smart Phone from his pocket. It was Basil! *Why won't he just give up,* Sam wondered.

BP: Yor K9 iz ugLE
SH: So R U!
BP: Yor ugLE 2!
SH: Yor a jerk
BP: BetA kEp yor eye on d K9
SH: BetA watch yor mouth!!!

19
Sticks And Stones – And Words *Can* Hurt!

Before Sam transferred to school in Misty Harbor, his schoolmates had been urged by their parents and teachers to ignore the fact that he was in a wheelchair. They had hoped that the kids would treat him the same as any other kid. Although the majority of the kids had complied with this request, Sam was sure they were being nice because they'd been told to. He'd forgotten that when some of Lily's band mates had taken a bus all the way to Boston to visit him in the rehabilitation center *before* he entered school, he had turned away and refused to speak to them. When they had tried again after Sam and his dad moved to Misty Harbor, he told his father, "I don't want to see them." Eventually, when their phone calls, texts and tweets went ignored, one by one, they gave up.

Although his classmates would still like to be friends with him, they were not sure what to say or do about his disability. They felt uncomfortable, not knowing what to do if he needed help maneuvering around in his wheelchair. Sam and his father had discussed this and he understood it, to a point. "Kids are freaked out by cripples," he'd told his father.

To make matters worse, Sam recently learned that Basil and Fingers had invented a guessing game to find out what Sam's legs looked like under the blanket that hid them from view.

"They zig zag," Fingers guessed.

"And they're purple," Basil added.

"GROSS!" chorused the Crabs. Thankfully, Sam had not heard what they were saying, he just knew it was disgusting.

Apparently, only kind, sensitive Lily knew how to get Sam's trust. They had met three summers ago while waiting in line for ice cream. Lily's mom and Sam's mom were childhood friends so it was only natural that they would set up a play date. From that moment on, Sam and Lily forged a friendship. Her honest, unassuming ability to call things as she saw them was one of her many endearing qualities. Lily had called, emailed, tweeted or texted Sam every day that he was in the hospital. When she had heard that he would be moving to Misty Harbor, she had promised herself that she would be his BFF. And Lily always kept her promises.

Although Sam was deeply embarrassed by his condition, and had never discussed it with Lily, finally, an event in school frustrated him to a point that he broke his silence. He'd wheeled himself into the auditorium to attend a crafts exhibition and had noticed everyone staring at him as he went from exhibit to exhibit. Sam stewed over this for a week.

Days later, when Lily came by to work on their video, he asked, "Why do people think I'm a freak, just because I'm in a wheelchair?"

Lily didn't blink an eyelash. "It's not you, Sam, Lily explained, "it's just normal for kids to be curious."

"What about you?" he asked timidly. "Are *you* curious to see my legs, because if you are …" Sam threw off the blanket that was always tucked firmly around his legs. Then he rolled up both pant legs. "There!" he announced defiantly. "This is what a freak looks like."

Lily remained frozen to the spot, unable to move, her eyes locked on Sam's.

"Look at them!" Sam insisted.

And she did.

Lily stifled a gasp when she saw trails of long scars on both of Sam's legs where he'd undergone several surgeries to repair his injuries. Some of the scars were purple, while others had begun to fade. Since he had not used his legs for over a year, his calf muscles had shrunk – his strikingly thin legs a stark contrast to his well-developed upper body.

"Pretty disgusting, huh?" he said, while waiting for Lily to say something – anything.

"Does it hurt?" she asked so innocently that Sam burst out laughing.

"I wish!" he replied, reaching for the blanket to cover his legs once more.

"Why do you want them to hurt?" Lily was perplexed.

"Because it would mean that I *feel* something, get it?" Sam said angrily. "My legs are numb."

"Why?" Lily asked simply.

"The doctors don't know."

Lily sat quietly, picked at a fingernail, thinking of what to say next. Actually, it came easily.

"What exactly happened to you?" Lily asked, settling in a chair, eager to learn some details.

Sam spun himself around in his wheelchair, and then pulled hard on the brake.

"There was an accident and my mom died," Sam stared directly at Lily, his eyes moist as he fought back tears.

"I know that," Lily said quietly. "Was it a car accident?"

"No." Sam shook his head slowly.

"What kind, then?"

"A bad kind." Sam took a deep breath, then opened his mouth as if he was about to say something. Instead, he released the brake and started toward his room.

"Come on, Lily," Sam said, "we've got a movie to edit."

Lily shrugged her shoulders. "Okay. You can tell me about the accident later, if you want to." *Or if you need to,* Lily thought.

20
And Action!

~

The following Saturday, Lily appeared carrying her tuba
and a plate of cookies. In her backpack she brought treats
for Daring. After feeding the dog she announced, "We're
going to play *Peter and the Wolf* for the Holiday Assembly,
and I have a big part!"

"That's cool, Lily, but why are you taking your tuba out
right now? We have work to do." Sam had been waiting
all week to wrap up this scene. He hoped Lily wasn't too
distracted.

"As soon as we film my part, I've got to practice while
you edit," Lily explained.

"Okay. You might want to wash Daring's slobber off your
face so we can get going," Sam said impatiently.

The location they'd chosen for the shoot had Lily standing next to the lighthouse with the ocean behind her. Sam
wanted to film the scene before the sun rose too high in the
sky.

Sam wheeled himself outside and directed Lily to her
position. Lily smoothed her nest of red hair, pinned the
microphone to the neck of her sweater, cleared her throat,

licked her lips and finally looked at the camera to wait for Sam's cue. "And action…" he said.

Using her best evening news voice, Lily reported, "The search for Mrs. Grady's cat has turned up lots of cats, but not her beloved Prince Charming. To help find her prized Siamese, a search team of volunteers has set out bowls of tuna fish in Prince Charming's favorite hiding places. This has been a real treat for Misty Harbor's cats that have been greedily emptying the bowls. Unfortunately, there's been no sign of Prince Charming."

"… And cut" Sam yelled, looking up from the camera and sounding like the hotshot movie director he was pretending to be. "Let's do it again, Lily. Try not to laugh when you talk about the town cats."

Daring, who'd been watching the production with interest, didn't know why there was all the fuss about some cat. If Prince Charming was anything like Gil and Phil, who'd been watching from the windowsill ever since they'd heard the word "cats," well. Never mind, that wasn't a very nice thought.

After a few more takes, Sam was satisfied. He and Lily packed up the equipment and returned to his room. While Sam plugged the camera into the computer, and prepared for the edit, Lily took out her tuba and practiced her part in *Peter and the Wolf*, over and over again. Although she'd certainly improved since Sam had first heard her play, she still needed a lot of practice. Her tooting set Shifty squawking like a mad man. Then, Gil and Phil decided it was time to strut and yowl, until for some unknown reason Shifty stopped squawking and began to sing "Let It Go…" It would have been almost funny except Shifty was singing in Mr. Harris' croadel, and the sound sent shivers up Daring's spine.

To add to the racket, Shifty imitated Archie speaking as the former President. "Y'all have fun," Shifty chirped over and over. And Archie repeated it.

And on and on and on it went until Sam pleaded, "STOP. YOU ARE DRIVING ME CRAZY!"

The dog shook and groaned until Sam turned to Lily and offered, "If you want to go home it's okay." What he didn't say was that the noise was making him crazy. Sam needed to take a break.

21
Here, Kitty Kitty
~

After Lily left for home, Sam clicked onto the webcam sites that were stationed throughout Misty Harbor. Sam's dad had volunteered to install the webcams, so Sam could see what was going on around town – and Archie's GPS signal could work off the webcams. Needless to say, the citizens of Misty Harbor, especially those who were housebound, were thrilled that they could travel virtually around town without leaving their homes.

As Sam used the webcams to search for Prince Charming, he zoomed in every time he saw a cat. "Boy, this town's got a lot of cats," he told Daring. Upon hearing the word "cats", Gil and Phil slinked in, and then positioned themselves at the corner of Sam's desk to watch the cats on the computer screen. Mackerel snored peacefully near Sam's bed.

Now alone in the living room, Shifty meowed non-stop, trying to lure the cats back to his domain. When that didn't work, he began calling Mackerel using Dr. Trout's voice – "Want a burger, Mackerel? Yum, yum, yum! Mackerel raised her head, open her big jaws, yawned, then stretched, and went back to his nap.

Furious at being ignored, Shifty was running out of ideas, until he remembered that he had just mastered Mr. Harris's voice.

"Archie, slice an orange for Shifty," he said, then waited patiently on his perch. The robot's head rotated from side to side as he scanned the room looking for Mr. Harris. Not seeing him, Archie went back to his programmed chores. After a few minutes, Shifty called out again. "Archie, bring Shifty an orange slice," he called. The robot marched to Shifty's cage and stood facing the bird.

"Y'all's a clever bird," Archie said.

"Y'all's a clever bird," Shifty mimicked.

"Y'all's teasing Archie," the robot said, his hologram flashing an embarrassed red.

"Teasing Archie, teasing Archie," Shifty crowed excitedly.

"No snacks for Shifty," Archie announced, and then turned toward the kitchen, leaving Shifty to swing madly in his cage.

After peering in to the living room to see what the commotion was, Sam turned his attention back to the computer. With one hand on the mouse and the other scratching Daring's head, Sam said, "Okay let's go to the corner of French and Garland."

Daring moved closer to the screen. *It's amazing,* she thought, *how things can fit inside that thing Sam is always looking at?*

"See that gray and white cat? That's Benicio. He belongs to the lady who used to cut my mom's hair," Sam said. Daring cocked her head. She wondered how the cat got in the monitor. Sam clicked the mouse on his keyboard to zoom in at Mooncusser Point in time to see a small gray cat chasing a big black dog. For a moment, Sam thought maybe it was Prince Charming, but it wasn't.

"Look, that's Tina Turner, Daring. She belongs to some big rock star that owns the house out on the point, but he doesn't come until summer. His name is Mick, something. My dad knows who he is," Sam explained, "Some guy stays there in the winter to take care of the place and feed the cat." Daring cocked her head, confused, but happy that Sam was having a long conversation with her.

On the webcam at the pier, Sam saw a huge Maine coon cat. Daring raised her eyebrows, then looked at Sam, as if to ask if it was Prince Charming. Sam laughed and scratched the top of her head. "No, that's Tiny, Daring. He must weigh twenty-five pounds. Look at how huge he is!" Just then, Tiny rolled over on his back and fell off the park bench he'd been snoozing on.

"Let's see what's going on over at Fairmount Park." Daring rubbed her head against Sam's knee, knocking the blanket to the ground. Then ever so gently, Daring sniffed at Sam's legs, and raised her head, her eyes never leaving Sam's face.

"I was in an accident, Daring, Sam explained, "just like you – sort of."

The dog stuck out her warm tongue. She looked longingly at Sam, panting hard, cocking her head.

"My mom died and I almost did, too," Sam confided.

Daring Dog began to lick Sam's shin, first one leg, and then the other – slowly, carefully, and oh, so lovingly.

Sam was taken completely off guard by the dog's devotion. For the first time since the accident, he left his legs uncovered so Daring could continue to lick him.

Sam said quietly, "You're a good dog, Daring, a good girl. I love your kisses and I love you, too." Sam patted Daring's head until he finally said, "That's enough, girl, I can't feel your licks, but it still makes me feel good."

Daring's drool covered both of Sam's legs. "Archie, bring me a towel," he called.

Archie appeared quickly, and passed a towel to Sam. Then, inexplicably, Archie turned to Daring and said, "Good dawg!" All the while, Mr. Harris watched from the doorway, stepping back so Sam wouldn't see him. Seeing the peaceful look on his son's face, Mr. Harris sighed deeply, and then he wiped away a tear.

22

Best Friends Forever

~

At breakfast the next morning, Sam was in great spirits. "Who's the best dog?" Sam asked Daring who was waiting for Sam next to his place at the table. The dog responded by raising the corners of her mouth, until several of the folds of her skin disappeared into one large fold. "Look, Dad, she's smiling at me!"

By gosh, she is, Mr. Harris shook his head in agreement.

"Look, Archie," Sam said. "Daring can smile."

"Happy dawg!" Archie exclaimed, "happy dawg!"

Daring thumped her tail. "See, Archie, she agrees."

"Happy dawg, happy dawg, happy dawg!"

Then Shifty joined in …

Being with Sam made Daring feel so warm, so cared about, so relaxed that she thought, *Maybe my life has changed, maybe I have a good future.* All she knew was that she never wanted to leave Sam. Being a great bloodhound tracker was a fine goal to have, but being a good friend to someone as kind as Sam was far more important. Daring had no clue that she could and should have both.

Later that day, Sam returned to webcamming, clicking rapidly, until he found something of interest.

"There's a hockey game on the pond," Sam said wistfully, as he explored with the webcam. He clicked to change direction and then found the Crabs having a snowball fight. He zoomed in time to see Fingers shove a fistful of snow down the back of Basil's jacket. "Good," he chuckled.

With another click of the mouse he focused on the skating rink where Mandy and Kelly were ice-skating. As more skaters appeared, he pointed them out to Daring.

"Those kids go to my school," he said, pointing to the screen.

"That's Kim and Jose with the scarf around his neck; there's Ahmed in the red ski jacket and I forget that girl's name – oh, it's Elisha." Sam tweeked the zoom until he was sure he could see Elisha shivering. "She looks like she's freezing to death – she just moved here from Israel." Sam laughed as Jose rubbed snow on Elisha's face. He laughed even harder when Elisha flipped Jose with one quick move. Suddenly, he stopped laughing, turned off the monitor, and sat quietly, his hands in his lap.

Something's wrong, Daring wondered. She didn't understand that Sam was sad because he couldn't be out there having fun with the kids. Gingerly, Daring moved closer, until she was resting her head on Sam's arm. Her heart was pounding in her chest because she could instinctively feel what Sam was feeling – that's how close they'd become. When Sam felt her head on his arm he bent down to kiss her forehead and scratch her chin.

Please don't stop, Daring wished, *this is better than wonderful. I can trust him. I really, really can!*

Sam's kiss on the top of her head sealed her trust in him, forever. *I could just float away,* she thought. Daring rubbed her head against his hand. *More, more,* she urged.

Sam scratched her behind her ears. *Oh, that feels great,* she sighed. He tickled her nose and tilted her head until she was close enough for Sam to kiss. Daring, who loved kissing Sam, let her tongue drop out, and then gently planted a long, drooly, sloppy, loving kiss on Sam's cheek.

"Good girl," Sam said softly. "I hope you know that you're my dog now."

Daring heeked.

"You're my girl, Daring, yes, you are!" Sam reached down and pulled her close, while stroking her back.

It's fair to say that dogs don't necessarily understand English, but in this case Daring was sure that she knew what Sam meant. Her heart raced and she smiled her goofy, wonderful smile from ear to ear.

"Let's go look at the mall." Sam said, turning back to his computer and clicking away. Click, click, click zoom! Sam and Daring had a front row seat at the mall just in time to see a man in black ... a flash of a silver-tipped boot ... then the screen went black!

The man had thrown something over the camera. In that moment, what was left of Daring's fur stood up straight as an arrow. A low growl rumbled from her throat.

"Hey, what's the matter girl?" Sam couldn't imagine what had gotten into her. Apparently, Daring had seen something that really upset her. Sam clicked from webcam to webcam, trying to locate the image that had caused Daring's reaction. No luck, whatever it was, it was gone now.

"Lime for tunch," Archie announced. He set out a plate of macaroni and cheese and a glass of chocolate milk on the table.

Archie's still got that glitch," Sam said when his father joined him. Mr. Harris reached over and pushed Archie's reset button.

"Bring a treat for Daring," Sam said, "please."

"Y'all want a biscuit?" Archie asked the dog.

Woof, thump, woof, thump.

Archie returned with some yummy peanut butter flavored dog biscuits that he dropped one at a time into Daring's open mouth.

"Dood gawg," Archie said, as his hologram lights flashed purple and pink. Mr. Harris pushed the reset button again, and then scratched his head.

"Dood gawg," Shifty chorused.

Daring didn't know what "dood gawg" meant, but she knew that it was a compliment. She barked a short baying sound at Archie, wagged her crooked tail, and then flopped at the robot's feet. At the same time, Archie reached out to Shifty's cage, and opened his hand to reveal a slice of an orange. The parrot grabbed it and then beaked rapidly until the treat disappeared.

"Good bird," the robot said softly.

"Good Archie," Shifty replied as he licked the remaining orange juice off his claw.

23
Maine's Most Wanted

~

S am and his father finished their errands with a trip to the pet store to buy a warm winter coat for Daring. The blue fleece coat Sam had chosen fit Daring perfectly and would provide protection for her against the howling winter wind and biting cold.

Not long after trying the coat on Daring, the wind picked up and snowflakes began to swirl.

"I'm glad we got this for her," Sam said, admiring the coat. "I can't stand how the wet snow feels like needles on my face and neither can Daring."

"I'll stoke the fire while Archie gets dinner on the table," Mr. Harris said. Gil and Phil were already snoozing by the woodstove.

"Can you take Daring out before it gets too cold," Sam asked as he put the coat back on the dog. "You better take Mackerel, too."

His father was happy to oblige. "Be quick about your business, dogs," Mr. Harris said as he put Mackerel's coat on and then hooked up their leashes. "It's a bit nippy out."

After a hearty dinner of meatloaf, mashed potatoes and salad, Sam, Mackerel and Daring shared a bowl of popcorn as they watched Sam's favorite television show – *Maine's Most Wanted.*

Sam announced, "Some day I'm going to be a professional detective, and you, Daring, are going to be my personal bloodhound. We will be the most famous crime fighting team in the world. You are a natural born tracker!"

What did Sam say? Daring wondered. *Was it something about crime fighting and tracking? I've heard those words before – when I was a baby."* Then Daring sneezed. *Oh yes,* she remembered... *the Masons, the Maine State trooper ...*

WHAT IF I FAIL? The thought hit Daring like a thunderbolt.

Daring dropped down on the rug. A worried look wrinkled her furrowed forehead. As if twenty wrinkles weren't enough, she now had twenty-four.

Sam texted Lily.

SH: Watch Mainc's Most wntd. Misty Harbor Toys 4 Tots drop off cNtR.

LC: Got h/w. Can't watch.

SH: jst 30 min. U & I R crime trackers.

LC: Tape it.

SH: K

LC: Mom says we can't txt 2night.

SH: wat did I do?

LC Nuttin. nEd 2 practiS.

SH: L8r

Sam and the dogs continued watching the program. The Toys for Tots drop-off center's security camera showed a blurry figure loading huge bags with toys. The image was so grainy there was no way the figure could be identified.

YET.

Suddenly, Daring began to rumble loudly, her ears twitched non-stop and she bared her teeth.

"Calm down, girl," Sam said.

"I told you not to give her so much popcorn," Mr. Harris scolded. He worried that Daring had a tummy ache, or that she'd have an accident inside the house while they were sleeping. Knowing that his father was probably right, Sam did what any kid his age would do. He ignored him.

"Hmmm, that was odd behavior for her," Mr. Harris thought. "Come here, Daring."

The dog obeyed and moved close to Mr. Harris.

"Let's see if this works on dogs," he said as he waved his WELLBEENER over Daring. The device made beeps and squishing sounds.

Mr. Harris squinted to see the numbers on his invention. "Whoopee," he exclaimed, "it works!"

"Is she okay?" Sam asked.

"She is just dandy," his dad proclaimed. "Now, let me try it out on Mackerel." Ever the scientist, Mr. Harris was lost to his invention as he waved his WELLBEENER over the aging bulldog. Just as it did with Daring, the WELLBEENER twirped and beeped. "Wait until I tell the good doctor!" he said proudly.

After saying goodnight to Sam, Mr. Harris put out fresh water for the animals, covered Shifty's cage despite the bird squawking in protest, and plugged in Archie's battery charger. Finished with his nightly routine, he sat in his over-stuffed chair and read for a while until it was almost midnight. When the clock struck twelve, Mr. Harris wrapped a heavy woolen scarf around his neck, pulled on a thick wool hat and down-filled jacket. He then entered the lighthouse chamber, as he did often because he loved the echoes from the thick stone walls as he tried to yodel. Sadly, since losing his wife, he was only able to manage a croadel no matter how hard he tried.

When he reached the top of the lighthouse, he entered the lantern room where the Misty Harbor light was making its rotations. Ten years ago, the powerful light was completely automated, eliminating the need for a lighthouse keeper. Still, Mr. Harris liked to check on it every so often.

In each section of the country, every lighthouse flashes with a different pattern. Before fancy navigational equipment like GPS and radar, ships used lighthouses to help figure out exactly where they were. Even now, with all that technology, it's nice to have a backup.

Despite the weather and strong wind, Mr. Harris stepped outside onto a narrow balcony to take a deep breath of the clean ocean air. He loved watching the churning ocean waves crash against the rocks upon which the cottage and lighthouse sat firmly.

Although the wind chill was almost unbearable, Mr. Harris took a moment to look to the sky. "He's getting better, Louise," he said, while focusing on a bright star. "The dog is good for him." After wiping a tear from his eye, he started to hum the first line of the old song he always sang to his wife … "*Every little breeze seems to whisper Louise …* "

He continued humming the song as he made his way back down the stairs and into the kitchen where he set the kettle to boil for a cup of tea. While waiting for it to whistle, he checked on Sam, who was sleeping soundly with Louise's Alaska hat tucked next to his chin, and his dog at the foot of his bed.

As Mr. Harris was leaving Sam's room, he turned to look at Daring, who opened one eye but didn't move.

"You're the best thing that's happened to this family in a long time, Daring."

Whop, whop, whop. Daring's tail signaled her gratitude.

24
House Call

~

The doorbell rang once, then played the tune of the day–
Beethoven's *Hallelujah Chorus.*

By the second "hallelujah" Daring started sneezing and
bouncing. Sam raced Archie to the front door, and opened
it to find Dr. Trout standing there.

"House call," she said cheerily, "I've come to check on
the troops."

"Would y'all like a cuppa tea?" Archie asked.

"Sure, no milk, one sugar." Dr. Trout took off her hat,
coat and scarf and did a quick check of the menagerie in
the living room. Then she settled into a comfortable chair
to talk with Sam. Gil and Phil leaped into her lap while
Mackerel plomped down at her feet.

"So, how's life with your new dog?" she asked, grinning
from ear to ear.

"Are you kidding, she's great!" Sam said, "but why does
she sneeze so much?"

"It just happens," Trout explained. "Once in awhile you
get an animal with allergies. Don't worry about it, Sam.
Usually, when one sense is weak, another sense is strong."

Sam relaxed. "She's really smart," he said with pride.

The vet nodded in agreement. Daring, who'd been listening, took a deep breath, puffed out her chest, slapped her tail on the floor and held her head up high.

Mr. Harris arrived from the kitchen carrying a plate of freshly sliced pumpkin bread, while Archie brought her tea.

"Can you believe what's going on in Misty Harbor?" Dr. Trout asked.

Mr. Harris scratched his head and nodded. "F-f-frankly, it's quite troubling. All of a sudden our sleepy little village of Misty Harbor is filled with crime!"

"I know," the vet agreed. "The Levins had their new television stolen and the Campbells are missing a package that was left on their front porch. It's disgusting."

"Disgusting," Archie repeated as he returned to the kitchen to make a cup of cocoa for Sam.

Sam's cell phone rang. It was Lily, who was rambling on so excitedly he could hardly understand her. "The holiday decorations from Fingers' house were stolen. And my mom just heard on the radio that the DVD player and all the DVDs have been stolen from the old people's home."

Sam was as shocked as everyone, but he couldn't help but want to put on his detective hat to solve the crimes. "I'll keep searching the webcams," he told Lily. "Want to come over?

"I wish I could, but I have orchestra practice," Lily explained.

"That's okay," Sam said, "I'll text you if I see anything."

"Well, I must get going," Dr. Trout said. I have a builder starting with the repairs and I'm still fighting with the insurance company."

"Just so you know, there's no rush in taking back your little pals, here," Mr. Harris said, nodding his head up and down, doing his best to offer his most generous smile.

"We've settled in to a comfortable existence and I think Daring enjoys having a member of her species around."

"That's really kind of you, Mr. Harris," Dr. Trout said gratefully. "I hate being a burden."

"Not at all," Mr. Harris assured her. "Here, let me help you with your coat," he offered. "I'll walk you to your truck."

As they walked together, Mr. Harris said, "Daring is a miracle, Dr. Trout. You have no idea what you have done for Sam."

"Call me Fanny Sunshine, please," she smiled warmly.

"All right, Fanny Sunshine – and call me Davidson, er … I mean Dave."

"Dave it is," said Fanny, while burrowing into her jacket. The wind was blowing steadily; icy froth from the waves began hitting their faces.

"As I was saying," Mr. Harris continued, "Daring is working miracles with Sam. He's beginning to come out of his shell; he actually smiles sometimes."

Dr. Trout nodded in agreement. "That's not surprising. A good dog can be good medicine."

Mr. Harris agreed. He'd seen a remarkable change in his son, and he knew it was due to Daring coming into their lives.

"You know, Sam seems to be different from when I first met him," Dr. Trout observed.

Mr. Harris thought for a moment. "I agree – well, he has a long way to go. It's been an uphill battle to get him to do his physical therapy. And he hates school. He's only made one friend – the little girl you met when they went to see Daring at your place …"

"I understand," the vet answered. She raised her red-mittened hand to make a point. "Slow down, be patient and have faith. Obviously, your boy has been through a lot."

"Oh, you've no idea –" Mr. Harris said, looking down at his boots.

Fanny Sunshine Trout was quiet for a moment. She had debated whether or not to say anything, but in the moment she made her choice.

"Now, you may find this hard to believe," she began, "but Finn and I are pretty convinced that there is a magical aura surrounding Daring. We both felt it during surgery. It's there, I can see it in her eyes."

Mr. Harris let out a little chuckle. "I'm a scientist, you know. I don't really believe in magic – but if you say so … who knows? It's a miracle that my son survived the accident, so maybe there is magic, after all."

When they reached the door of her truck, a gust of icy wind blew another spray of salt water, stinging Dr. Trout's cheeks. "If you want to continue this conversation, you'll need to hop in my truck."

Mr. Harris smiled while pulling up the hood of his jacket. "I really should be getting back to my chores," he answered. "You're very kind, Fanny Sunshine Trout. I just want you to know that I am eternally grateful."

Dr. Trout hopped into the driver's seat and turned the key in the ignition. "Just have faith, Dave. I truly believe that we don't choose our pets – they choose us! Daring has come into Sam's life for a reason. Wait and you'll see."

When Mr. Harris turned to walk back to the house, he noticed Sam and Daring with their noses pressed to the window. Could it be that his son –*and his dog*– were SMILING?

25

Move Over, Sherlock

~

That night, Sam put on his detective cap. When he clicked on the town pier's webcam, he caught his breath, then zoomed in.

"OMG, Daring!!! It's that guy with those boots! He's pulling a tarp over something in the back of his truck."

Sam dialed 911 on his cell phone. Chief Butters had been watching the *Home Shopping Network* and was punching in his credit card number when the call came in. "There's a guy acting suspicious at the town pier," Sam said breathlessly. "Hurry!"

Butters swiveled in his chair to check the wall of webcam monitors. He saw Cade pull the tarp tightly over what looked like the size and shape of a flat screen television.

"*Oh, yeah, baby, Copper and Beech are five minutes away,*" he said to himself as he picked up the police radio.

"Get over to the town pier right away, boys," he shouted over the radio. "We've got him – grey or black pickup, parked near the end of the pier. It's a slam, dunk!" Butters smiled from ear to ear. Then he sat back to watch the arrest on the monitor.

Sam's heart thumped as he zoomed in to watch, but Cade had his hat pulled down low on his forehead. Sam couldn't see his face.

"Rats," Sam cussed. He couldn't identify him. A flash of silver caught Sam's eye. "Daring, wake up," Sam said, nudging the napping dog. But by the time Daring finished a long, satisfied stretch, Cade had cranked his ignition and sped away.

"NO, NOT YET! WAIT!" Butters yelled at the monitor. He grabbed the radio again, but Copper and Beech had the sirens going full blast and couldn't hear him.

A minute later, the police arrived. They saw a dark-colored truck parked at the end of the pier. Sam watched over the webcam as two policemen exited the squad car. They hunkered down, guns drawn, and crept to the parked truck.

"Police!" Sgt. Copper yelled, "Raise your hands and come out of the car." Sgt. Beech shone a flashlight into the car nearly blinding the eyes of a local fisherman. The man was startled so badly that his lips moved up and down, but no sound came out.

"Darn it! It's just Fred Smiley," Sgt. Copper groaned. Smiley crawled out of the car, rubbing his eyes.

"Well, did you see anything?" Sgt. Copper asked?

"See what?" Fred Smiley asked, confused. "The fish aren't biting so I thought I'd take a snooze before heading home."

"Sorry," Sgt. Copper apologized.

Meanwhile, Cade was speeding up the Maine Turnpike, until coming to his exit that he took on two wheels. He was safe once again. *At this rate, I'll be sold out and heading out west right after Christmas,* he thought excitedly.

26
Having A Bad Day
~

"I just heard the news; there was another robbery last night," Mr. Harris announced at breakfast.

"I know, Dad, I saw it on the webcam. I called the police but they got there too late."

Mr. Harris folded the newspaper he'd been reading. "That's too bad, Sam, but good detective work. Are you all ready for school?"

Sam sat silently, pushing his scrambled eggs around his plate.

"I hate that place," he mumbled.

"Do you want to talk about it?" Mr. Harris asked.

"The kids are stupid."

"Do we use that word, Sam?"

"Ok. The kids are dumb."

"Sam!"

Sam pushed himself away from the table. "Ok, they're MEAN, Dad. They make fun of me, they think I'm a dork – a, a cripple!"

Mr. Harris was mortified. No wonder Sam was so miserable. Mr. Harris slapped his hand on the table. "I can put a stop to that!"

"DON'T YOU DARE! YOU WILL MAKE IT WORSE!"
Sam exploded.

Mr. Harris scratched his head, shrugged his shoulders,
and then quietly asked, "What do you expect me to do, Sam?
I can't sit by and watch my son be deprived of his education
because he is being bullied."

Sam fidgeted with his fingers. "Let me deal with it, Dad.
Pretty soon they'll find someone else to pick on. Okay?"

Mr. Harris fretted and returned to his newspaper. But it
was not okay. He was just not sure what to do about it.

"What's for dinner tonight, Archie?" Sam asked as he
pulled on his hat and wrapped a scarf around his neck.

"Y'all requested spaghetti and meatballs with lots of
Parmesan cheese on top," Archie answered, while at the
same time, Mr. Harris said "Steak and potatoes."

Sam shook his head and laughed. The mood had
changed. "Hey, you programmed him, Dad. Anyway, I vote
for spaghetti."

"Fine," Mr. Harris grumbled. "Archie, print out a shopping list for me, will you please."

The lights on Archie's chest screen flashed tomato red,
green pepper green and onion yellow. When the lights
stopped flashing, a piece of paper slid out of a kind of ATM
slot with the ingredients and recipe for *lasagna*.

Mr. Harris scratched his head. "Hmmm. Lasagna will be
fine, Archie. Thank you anyway," Mr. Harris said. "I'll work
the bugs out of your programming soon."

"This recipe comes from R-r-r-roma," Archie said, rolling his "r's". His GPS appeared on his message screen. Sam
and Mr. Harris watched as Google earth zoomed over the
Atlantic, slowed down near the Mediterranean, and stopped
in Rome, Italy.

"Arrivederci! Y'all have a dood bay," Archie said, and then proceeded to clear the table.

"You have physical therapy at 3:30 today, Sam. I'll pick you up at school," Mr. Harris said as he and Daring hurried along, pushing Sam to the bus stop at the end of the breakwater.

A deep frown appeared on Sam's face. "I'm not going any more."

Mr. Harris knew Sam didn't like his therapy, but he had to stand firm and not let him give up. It was Sam's only hope if he were ever to walk again. "It's not negotiable, Sam. You have a ways to go yet, but you'll see results if you let them do their job and work with them."

"I said no," Sam sneered. "I AM DONE!"

Daring watched the exchange with confusion. *I don't know what Dad said to Sam but he made him angry. I wish I could fix this and make Sam happy,* Daring thought.

"I'll be at your school at 3 o'clock, Sam," Mr. Harris said forcefully. "How about if I bring Daring to your session?"

Sam was about to argue, until he thought about it. Maybe having Daring with him would make his therapy session go by faster. Or maybe Daring would protect him and scare the therapist from pushing him hard to make him do something that he COULDN'T DO, ANYWAY.

"Okay?" Mr. Harris asked, as his furry eyebrows rose over his glasses.

Sam shook his head. "Okay."

Today's therapy session was in the warm pool. Although Sam couldn't feel his legs, the warm water felt good on his chest and back. Actually, aquatic therapy wasn't so bad.

As he worked his way across the pool with the help of his therapist, Daring followed back and forth on the pool deck. Finally tired, Daring laid down, content to follow Sam with her eyes.

When the session ended, Mr. Harris could tell that his brilliant idea to bring Daring along had worked.

"How about I ask if Daring can come to all of your sessions from now on?" Mr. Harris asked cheerfully.

"I know what you're doing, Dad," Sam answered. "It's not going to work."

"You're not going to give up, Sam. I'm not going to let you." Mr. Harris clenched the steering wheel in his gloved hands. "I mean it, Sam. You are going to walk some day, it's just going to take time."

Sam ignored him.

At a stoplight on their way home, Daring growled and barked ferociously upon seeing the person in the truck next to him. Sam, who was playing with his Smart Phone, ignored Daring. So, to get Sam's attention, Daring whimpered and pressed her body against him.

"What is it, girl?" Sam asked a little annoyed.

"Heek, argh, heek," Daring answered.

Daring turned back to look at the man in the truck, and she bared her teeth. Sam noticed.

AND SO DID CADE. *I just saw a ghost*, he thought. *That can't be Daring.*

Meanwhile, Sam hit the video icon on his Smart Phone, and started shooting.

Whoa, Cade thought and then he realized that Daring recognized him. *And the kid has a camera!*. When the light changed, Cade sped off before Sam was able to see the numbers on the license plate. It was another lucky getaway for Cade. And maybe not so lucky for Daring.

All the way back to his grandmother's house, Cade obsessed over the fact that Daring was alive. *After the trouble that I went through for that dog, I should get payback,* Cade ranted to himself. It's too bad he wasn't smart enough to just let sleeping dogs lie.

Sam texted Lily:
SH: Daring came 2 PT 2day
LC: Kewl
SH: thN werd n d car l8r
LC: ?
SH: She growled @ a guy n a truk
LC: wot wz he doing?
SH: w8N 4 d grEn lite
LC: Werd
SH: Y. Werd.
LC: Webcamming 2night?
SH: 2 much h/w
LC: Me 2

The lasagna was delicious and Sam ate heartily.

"Excellent meal, Archie," Mr. Harris said. As the robot did the dishes, he sang an old Italian song, "Volare, o, o … cantare ….o, o, o, o." And then Archie's computer program stuck on "o, o, O, o …"

"Quiet!" Mr. Harris yelled at Archie.

"Archie is quiet," the robot answered, the singing stopped.

Mr. Harris made a batch of popcorn, and then looked for the jar of caramel to melt and drizzle on top of the popcorn. It was one of Sam's favorite treats. He opened the cabinet where it should be and it wasn't there.

"Is there any caramel?" he asked Archie.

The robot didn't answer, and continued doing the dishes.

"IS THERE ANY CARAMEL?" Mr. Harris asked, much louder.

Archie turned to Mr. Harris. "Archie is quiet," he announced, then went back to doing the dishes. Apparently, Mr. Harris had programmed *feelings* into Archie. That being the case, even *robots* don't like to be yelled at.

"I'm sorry I yelled, Archie."

"That is an apology!" Archie said. "The caramel is on the counter." Archie was programmed to know that Sam always gets a treat after physical therapy.

Feeling a bit silly, Mr. Harris opened the jar of caramel and placed it in the microwave. Then he warmed up some apple cider for Sam and himself and put cinnamon sticks in their mugs. "Drink up and then it's time to hit the books, Sam."

"I KNOW, DAD."

Mr. Harris then plopped a few dog treats on the table next to Sam.

"No popcorn for Daring or Mackerel, Sam. Just milk bones."

"Aw."

"Seriously, Sam," Mr. Harris said. "I'm pooped and just want to relax."

Why is it that when a parent says something like that things go wrong quickly? No sooner had Mr. Harris flopped down in his chair and put his feet up on the ottoman, than Daring began a major sneezing fit. At one point she sneezed so hard that she smashed into the coffee table, knocking over the gooey, sticky, bowl of popcorn.

Sam couldn't help himself. He began to laugh so hard that he shook. Unable to understand what all the fuss was about as Mr. Harris and Archie cleaned up the mess, Daring and Mackerel devoured every stray morsel they could lick up, ignoring the caramel goo on their tongues.

27
Memories

~

As Sam got ready for bed, Mr. Harris bent down to empty Archie's vacuum cleaner bag. "It's amazing how a bowl of popcorn can have so many kernels, Archie," he said to the robot.

While on his knees, Mr. Harris' eyes settled on a brown cardboard box next to the curio cabinet. He remembered how sad he was the night that he filled the box to put away his wife's treasures. Sam had pleaded with him to do so and cried until he finally gave in. That was months ago. *Maybe now?* Mr. Harris wondered.

After pausing for a moment, Mr. Harris slid the precious box from its resting place. He struggled to think of a way to express his feelings, but words did not come. Instead, he patted Daring's head and smiled at Sam, who had just come from brushing his teeth.

"I'm glad you have her," Mr. Harris said.

"Me, too."

When Mr. Harris lifted the lid of the box, Sam glanced in his direction, and then looked away. He clicked the television remote button. *I'm not ready for this*, he thought as his heart twinged and he began to sigh. Yet deep inside, he wanted his dad to continue.

Mr. Harris was nervous. He took a deep breath before he removed the wrapping from the first item, an Eskimo doll that his wife had brought from a remote village near Nome, Alaska. The doll wore a traditional fur parka and boots; a pretty smile was painted on her face. Not surprisingly, the doll's face resembled Louise Harris's when she was a young girl.

The daughter of an Inuit father and an English mother, Louise Harris had been a stunning mixture of her heritage. She had inherited her father's lustrous dark hair and coloring and her mother's cornflower blue eyes. When Davidson Harris had stumbled into her in their college cafeteria, he was met with laughter and a gentle nudge, even though he'd made her drink spill into her salad. From that day on, they had spent the rest of their time together. They shared the same sense of humor, good study habits and inquisitive minds. They had married upon graduating, then moved to Massachusetts to pursue their graduate degrees – his in computer science, hers in marine biology. Sam was their only child.

With a lump in his throat and one eye watching Sam's reaction, Mr. Harris placed the doll in the curio cabinet.

Sam put his tablet aside and watched, sadly, as his father continued to unwrap his mother's treasures.

"I-I could use some help," Mr. Harris said, clearing his throat.

Sam rolled his wheelchair closer, then reached into the box and unwrapped a small package containing a piece of fossilized walrus tusk. He handed it to his father who placed it next to a small stone carving of a wolf.

"No Dad," Sam corrected him. "It goes next to the Eskimo doll." Mr. Harris nodded, and then set the tusk in its rightful place – the place where it used to be before the accident and before their move to Maine.

Sam's lower lip trembled as he struggled to control himself. Finally, months of his locked away feelings escaped. Heavy tears slid down his cheeks.

Seeing Sam's distress, Daring jumped up to lap Sam's face, but he pushed her away. Unfazed, Daring returned, trying to lick at Sam's tears.

"Let it out, Sam," Mr. Harris urged. He reached for Sam's hand and for a change Sam didn't pull it away.

"Archie, please make us some hot chocolate," Mr. Harris said, not taking his eyes off Sam.

"Y'all want marshmalla?" the robot drawled.

"Sam?"

Sam dried his eyes and wiped his nose. "Double marshmallow for me."

"That's a lot of sugar," Archie warned.

"It's okay," Mr. Harris said, "Let's do this together, son. He reached into the carton and passed Sam another item to unwrap.

"Where did she get this, Dad?" Sam asked, as he held a sculpture in the shape of a whale's tail carved from polished white stone.

Mr. Harris smiled warmly. "She brought that back from a trip to Iceland before you were born."

"Was that when she saved the beluga whale?"

"That's right, son. She directed a whole rescue operation."

"The whale was tangled in fishing nets, right?"

"Absolutely. So when she left, the fisherman whose nets had entangled the whale, gave her this sculpture." Mr. Harris remembered how excited his wife had been when she returned.

Sam nodded his head and smiled. "Yeah, I remember her telling me about it."

Next, Sam unwrapped a delicate silver dogsled attached to six silver dogs. Sam knew the story behind this treasure but asked about it anyway.

"We spent our honeymoon traveling through Alaska," Mr. Harris began, after taking off his glasses and wiping away a tear. "Of course, your mother never took a real vacation, so she combined our honeymoon with an opportunity to study humpback whales."

Sam absent-mindedly began to play with the silver whale's tail that hung from a narrow chain around his neck.

Mr. Harris continued, "We had to travel by dogsled to some of the places she wanted to visit, so when we got back to Ketchikan I saw this in a souvenir store down by the pier. I was going to give it to her on our first anniversary. Instead, I gave it to her when you were born, in fact ..."

"Okay, you can stop there, Dad."

Mr. Harris laughed heartily. He remembered that Louise had told Sam that particular trip was very romantic. That was the reason why Mr. Harris gave her the gift at Sam's birth, instead of waiting for their anniversary.

Sam was smiling as he examined the little sculpture.

"You like hearing these stories, don't you," his father smiled.

Sam nodded and sighed. "Yeah."

After taking a break to enjoy their hot chocolate, they continued to unwrap dozens of small sculptures of wolves, bears and frogs, all carved by the Inuit people who lived near the Arctic. Their homeland stretched from the northeastern tip of Russia, across Alaska and northern Canada.

At the bottom of the box, Sam found the special package he'd been looking for. Very carefully, he unwrapped a long, thin package. It held an American eagle's feather, a souvenir from their trip to Haines, Alaska.

"I found this when we went to watch the eagles fish for salmon," Sam said while examining the feather. He ran his finger from its quill to the tip, nearly a foot in length. Suddenly, he felt a wisp of warm air swirl around him. Flecks of gold seemed to glisten in the air. He felt a faint rush of something smoothing the cowlick on top of his head. He lifted his shoulders and tilted his head from side to side.

"That tickles, stop, Dad. How are you doing that?"

"Doing what?" Mr. Harris asked as he carried their empty mugs to the kitchen. Sam looked around. Daring was at his feet, Archie was setting the table, Shifty lofted on a perch in his cage; the cats and Mackerel were curled in front of the fireplace. *Oh well,* Sam thought, *I must have imagined it.*

28
Seeing is Believing
~

Before going to bed, Sam spent some time scanning the webcams as he searched for Prince Charming. He was deeply engrossed in studying each frame for any sign of the cat when suddenly, Daring started making a fuss, heeking and running around in a circle. Daring kept leaping around the room, sneezing and barking. "Ow-woof!" She was going wild!

"Calm down," Sam said to his agitated dog.

KER-PLUNK!

"HEEK!" Daring answered. "HEEEEEEEK!"

"Stop it, Daring. I'm busy," Sam said. He was annoyed by the dog's behavior.

"HEEEEEEEEEEK."

Sam pushed away from the computer and picked up his Smart Phone.

SH: U shud hav cn her, Lily.

LC: Why>

SH: She wz growling, thN pushing in2 me, llk she wz trying 2 TLK.

LC: R Usure?

SH: UwouldB2 f U wer ther

As Lily and Sam texted each other, Daring stopped her antics and stood in front of the computer monitor in time to see Cade breaking into the school. Sam was too intent on texting Lily to notice that Daring was leaping five feet in the air.

"Woof, woof," she jumped higher and higher; kerplunked harder and harder. Six feet, seven feet, TEN! KERPLUNK!

"Shush, Daring," Sam said.

"AWWW-OOOOF!"

"What the heck IS IT?" Sometimes Daring chose the wrong moments to need Sam's attention.

Finally, Sam looked in the direction of the other monitor. It was focused on the school webcam.

"There's nothing there, Daring," Sam said, "It's just my school."

"Heek," Daring whimpered.

Daring flopped back down on her bed. She thought, *It's him – I know it!*

Early the next morning, Principal Duncan was surprised to see the school janitor waiting outside the building. He waved his arms frantically and began shouting when the principal got out of his car.

"All of the computers are gone from the library!" he shouted.

Principal Duncan raced inside to see for himself. When he reached the library, his heart sunk. The school's brand new computers had disappeared, leaving only their power cords behind. "Call the police," he murmured to the janitor.

This was a huge setback for the students who had been able to work on their projects while at school. Basil wouldn't tell anyone, but he was actually fascinated with the ocean, especially how waves were formed and he preferred learning about it online on a fast computer like the ones at school.

At home, they had a weak signal from their cable company and it could take minutes to download a file.

Fingers' father wouldn't let him have a guinea pig until he learned how to care for it, so he'd been looking for YouTube videos to teach him pet care – and he was getting extra credit for making it his project.

Unfortunately, it could be at least a year before the town could afford to replace the equipment.

Mr. Harris had a plan.

"I can network some of my old computers and give them to the school," he told Sam. "And I'll call my friends at the Media Lab to see if they have any that they're about to recycle. They do that all the time."

"Okay," Sam barely uttered.

His father took a deep breath. "Is something wrong?"

"No, I mean – it's good to get some computers for the school, just don't make it a *big deal*. Okay?"

"Okay, but wouldn't you want your classmates to know that your father was helping out?"

"NO. THAT'S THE POINT."

Mr. Harris sighed long and hard. He just didn't understand Sam anymore.

The next night as Sam and his father were busy in the little workroom at the back at the house, upgrading software and assembling computers for the school, Daring stayed in Sam's room. He watched the computer screen and saw Cade walking slowly past a camera store.

"Owwwwwww-ooofffff," she growled low and deep. Daring paced the room, her nose twitched, and she barked and barked until Sam wheeled in to check on her. Daring looked once at Sam, and then ran toward the computer. She sat very erect, staring at the screen.

"What's up, girl? Sam did nothing, just looked confused. So Daring did it again and again, running back and forth from Sam to the computer screen until she tripped over her ears.

Sam could see that she was really agitated. "Calm down, Daring, come on out to the workroom and be with us," Sam said stroking her head in an attempt to calm her. When Sam turned his wheelchair to leave, Daring tried to communicate one more time. She shook her head, and her long ears flopped over her eyes. Next, she started a sneezing fit.

"How about some fresh air?" Sam suggested.

Sam opened his window wide enough for a salty breeze to whip the curtains and fill the room. Then he returned to the workroom.

Maybe I'm wrong, Daring thought.

But I know I'm RIGHT!

She looked at the monitor again. *Yes, it's that man I used to live with.* The fur across her spine stood up straight. Her nose twitched madly. She shook her head so hard that her ears slapped the sides of her face. *I must do something,* she thought.

BUT WHAT?

Then it came to her, a fuzzy memory, flickering images that are shrouded in a shimmering veil. An image forms in her mind, a tiny creature whispering in her ear … "You can track *my* way. I'll show you how." …

Daring looked at the open window. *Ready, set, go,* she told herself.

TRACK!!!

Without hesitating, she jumped through the window, did a somersault in the air, and landed snout down in the snow.

29
Up, Up And Away!

~

"*Achoo!*" After a hearty sneeze, Daring cleared the snow from her nose. She tilted her head to the sky, her nostrils twitching madly, eyes scanning, until the thick folds of her mouth curled up in a smile. She closed her eyes and her dreams during surgery flashed before her. *I'm confused*, she thought, *but what the heck, it doesn't hurt to try.*

Nervous on her first try, Daring jumped pretty high, landing spread-eagled in a snowdrift. *Hmm*, she thought. *Not so good.* She surfaced with a face full of snow. "*Achoo!*" She snorted out the snow. Again, the images from her dreams flashed in her mind. *Oh, I have to jump higher,* she realized, only this time she became tangled in the holiday lights that were strung from the boathouse to the roof, and landed even harder in a snowdrift. *Getting there,* she told herself. When she dug her way out, a red light flashed from her nose and a green light blinked from her tail.

On her next try, she landed too close to a picket fence where Mr. Harris had spent hours draping garlands of holly – which now trailed behind Daring. At this point most people, to say nothing of dogs, would probably give up. Not Daring. She tried really hard again, really, really hard. And she crash-landed on the rowboat that Mr. Harris had just painted with expensive, marine-grade, and hard-to-remove paint. Undaunted, despite her now electric blue feet, she tried again. She concentrated really hard, then let out a whopper of a sneeze, which resulted in a higher bounce, and then….down. She knocked over the snowman, emerged wearing his hat and carrying his carrot nose in her mouth. Tracking blue paint over the snow, wearing flashing lights, a garland of holly, and the snowman's hat and nose, she tried one last time.

Daring closed her eyes and concentrated harder than before until suddenly, the image from her dream was in front of her eyes. *I can see that gold thing better now. It's part bird, part woman,* Daring realized.

"I'm Ukat, the goddess of good luck," the golden image said circling Daring's head.

Daring studied what Ukat was doing with her arms and legs. "Follow me," Ukat urged. Daring shuffled over to stand by her side.

Ukat lead Daring through her first steps very slowly. "It's kind of like the *Hokey Pokey*," she said.

Hmmm, Daring thought. *I don't think I know Hokey Pokey.*

Ukat tucked her wings by her side.

"Watch my feet," she said. "You put your right foot in," she assumed a graceful pose. Daring, who didn't know left from right immediately put her left foot … out. The tiniest of giggles tinkled from the magical creature.

"Let's try again," Ukat said gently, repeating the gesture for Daring to study.

Oh, the OTHER foot. Daring put her right foot in, but she lost her balance and fell on her face.

Unfazed, Ukat urged her to keep trying. "It's okay. Use your left foot. Let's do it again." Finally, after dozens of tries, Daring Dog realized *By George, I've got it!*

"And now, my friend. You are ready to learn to fly!"

With Daring's eyes glued to her, Ukat demonstrated the fine art of flying. She dipped and swooped, swerved and landed as dainty as the tiniest ballerina. As Daring tried to imitate her style, Ukat stood patiently until she was satisfied that Daring was ready to try on her own.

Daring bent a little deeper, pushed a little harder, and imagined herself being able to fly. Vrooom! *Wow, I just jumped as high as the top of the lighthouse!* This time her long floppy ears billowed out in slow motion and her jowls drooped lower. Braver now, Daring paid close attention as Ukat fluttered above her head. The goddess was pointing to her legs. *Ah-hah, Left foot in, right foot out,* Daring realized. Another try and woof! Daring was wobbly and doing flips but she was F-L-Y-I-N-G!!! Daring circled the lighthouse, and then ker-plunked on the boathouse roof.

Thanks Ukat, you rock! Daring thought, wagging her tail to show her appreciation, to say nothing of her excitement.

By the time Mr. Harris stepped outside to see what the clatter was about, Daring was up, up, and away flying to the end of the breakwater. Half asleep, Mr. Harris scratched his head and went back inside. A few seconds later, Daring landed behind the lighthouse.

She shed the lights, garland and hat, got her blue feet into perfect position and was soaring! The salty air filled her lungs. She swooped up and swooped down, skimming the surface...and back again.

I can be the best tracker in the world now!

30
Remember Me?

~

The next morning, when he opened the front door to fetch the morning newspaper, Mr. Harris was upset to see their garland of holly and holiday lights strewn across a snow bank.

"Darn!" Mr. Harris cussed. "How the heck did our holly garlands come loose so quickly?" A path of deep footprints about the size of Daring's appeared nearby. "Da-ring!" he called. He suspected that the dog had something to do with this.

"Daring, how'd you get those blue feet?" Mr. Harris asked when he caught up with Daring and Sam as they waited for the school bus. Sam wondered, too.

Daring just wagged her tail, cocked her head to the side, and then gave her best bloodhound smile to Sam as he waved to her through the window.

As soon as the school bus drove off, Mr. Harris said gruffly, "Inside, Daring."

"Dawgs will be dawgs," Archie said when Mr. Harris threw a fit.

"But after all the work!" Mr. Harris exclaimed, "I'm just, plain furious."

"Explain your sentence, please." Archie's response to Mr. Harris' complaint hadn't been programmed.

Mr. Harris' face was red with anger and frustration. "Stop it, Archie, you know what I mean!"

Archie stopped moving, turned his head toward Mr. Harris and reminded him, "Y'all are arguing with a robot!" When it dawned on Mr. Harris that he was, indeed, HAVING AN ARGUMENT WITH A ROBOT, he grabbed his hat, coat, scarf and mittens and trudged off for a nice long walk.

"Y'all have a nice day," Archie said from the doorway.

"HARR-UMPH," was Mr. Harris' reply.

Later that evening after Sam fell asleep, Daring sat waiting, her eyes locked on the computer screen. Sure enough, Cade appeared but this time Daring was ready. In the back of her mind she heard the Masons' song … *"I'm gonna getcha, I'm gonna getcha!"* Yes! *I am gonna getcha … and be a crime-fighting dog. A tracker!*

With the tip of her nose, Daring lifted Sam's bedroom window and then slipped outside. She was going to TRACK! By her breeding and instinct, she put her nose to the snowy ground, as she'd seen her littermates do so many times. But for Daring, well, her nose didn't work the way other dog's noses worked. *I can't ever seem to get a good whiff, but I can see just fine,* she reminded herself. *I can do it,* she told herself as she worked up her courage. *I can, I can, I can!*

No more sniffing the ground for this bloodhound, she thought.

Daring took a deep breath, forced a hard sneeze and made two false starts, landing sideways one time, upside down the next. But on her third try, she took off like a rocket. In no time she was soaring over Misty Harbor, turning left and right, using her crooked tail as a rudder, rising up and flying low, until she got her bearings. *I know where I am,* Daring realized. *I'm gonna getcha!*

What a night it was for Daring, swooping around Misty Harbor as the town slept, until finally, as she was about to turn back to the lighthouse, she spotted him ... *Oh, oh, oh – it's him!* It was Cade, who was just about ready to get into his truck.

Gotcha! Daring felt her heart pounding in excitement. First, she buzzed Cade, managing to knock him off his feet. Next, she dive-bombed him and took a bite out of the seat of Cade's pants. *Hah! Gotcha good that time!*

Furious, Cade tried to grab her, but she flew way above his head.

"Get back here, Daring! You belong to me!" Cade jumped in his truck thinking he could track the dog while he was driving. He lost sight of her very quickly.

"Dang!" he screamed, pounding his fist on the steering wheel. "I'll get you next time," he said aloud.

Only on his drive home did it dawn on Cade that the dog appeared to be flying.

"I must've dreamed up the whole deal," he said to himself. "But I could swear it was Daring!"

When Daring returned home, not having mastered the fine art of landing, she crashed headfirst into the wall beneath Sam's window. Sam was about to get out of bed to check out the thump when he saw Daring hoisting herself through the window.

"Hey girl. You don't need to go through the window to go to the bathroom. I'll have my dad put in one of those doggie doors so you can go out whenever you need to." Sam had no idea...

A few nights later, Daring disappeared again through Sam's open window. Only this time, Sam awakened in the middle of the night after having a bad dream. Daring was not in her bed. *She's just gone outside for a moment,* he assumed.

Unable to get back to sleep, and still waiting for Daring, Sam logged onto the Misty Harbor webcams. With a click, he saw the town pier; another click and he was at Fairmont Park. Then he focused toward Garland Street. What's that? A flash of silver, he zoomed in and whoa! Sam couldn't believe his eyes. "Omg, it's Daring!" he said breathlessly. As Sam watched in disbelief, Daring swooped down, her long ears trailing behind, and she buzzed Cade who was yelling and screaming at her while trying to flee with his loot. Sam began shaking his head, wondering if he was still asleep. It couldn't be true. Quickly, he clicked "save". In case he was dreaming, he'd look at the video clip in the morning.

Sam sat at the window for a few minutes waiting for Daring to return. When he started to fall asleep in his wheelchair, he returned to his bed. As his eyes began to close he heard the now familiar thud outside his window. With one eye open, he watched Daring hoist herself through the window. Daring looked at Sam, and then did a dog tiptoe to her bed, careful not to awaken Sam. In a second, she knocked over a stack of books and a rack of DVDs, setting off a clatter loud enough for Mr. Harris to call out to Sam from his bedroom.

"I'm fine, Dad," Sam answered without letting on to Daring that he'd seen her. Instead, he closed his eyes and let his imagination run wild. Boy did he have plans!

31

The Dynamic Duo

~

The next night Sam was ready. He closed his door and latched the lock on his window so Daring couldn't make her escape.

When Daring padded over to the window, Sam popped up in bed, threw back the covers. He was dressed in his jeans and a sweater. In no time he pulled his coat, hat, scarf and mittens out from under his pillow and was ready to go.

"I know what you've been doing and I want you to take me with you," he said as he zipped up his down jacket.

Daring cocked her head to the side, played dumb at first, and then wagged her tail. *I don't know how this will work, but I'll do anything for Sam, she* reasoned.

"I've got it figured out, girl, just watch me and be real quiet."

Sam grabbed his cell phone, and was super cautious as he wheeled outside and over to the boathouse. Earlier in the day, he'd stashed an old parasail and two harnesses in the corner.

"Come on, girl," Sam said, "stand still." He strapped one harness on Daring, the other on himself. Then Sam attached his wheelchair, using very strong bungee cords.

Finally, he clipped a webcam onto Daring's collar. Suddenly, Sam heard a noise and both he and Daring froze in their tracks. Once he realized it was probably just a wave slapping against the rocks, he relaxed.

I might be crazy, Sam thought, *but I know this is going to work!* Sam took a deep breath, screwed up his courage and then leaned forward in his wheelchair. He's ready!

"Go as fast as you can, Daring, and then we'll fly together!"

Daring looked at Sam and studied his face. She didn't move.

"Daring, we're going to fly together, girl, you and me! You just have to run faster than you ever have and it will work. You'll see! Now, GO GIRL!"

Daring raced along the length of the breakwater, let out a humongous sneeze, took a major bounce, nearly to the top of the lighthouse, and then, magically, the wind filled Sam's parasail and together it was liftoff!

"Awesome!" Sam shrieked. This was more than he could ever have imagined.

Oh boy, Daring thought, *I better fly low so if he falls he won't fall far.*

Daring skimmed low over the breakwater. "Incredible!' Sam screamed. "I love it!!!"

Sam and Daring flew from the lighthouse to the mainland and back. They circled over the Misty Harbor neighborhoods where Cade had been before, but there was no sight of him. Sam knew who Daring was looking for.

"It's okay, girl. Let's go home now," Sam yelled above the wind.

Daring raised her tail and shifted it a little to the left. In a matter of seconds, the lighthouse came into view. Daring slowed down, and Sam fell on top of a soft mound of snow. *Oh no, I've hurt him,* she feared.

"It's okay, girl," Sam whispered, "practice makes perfect." As Sam maneuvered his wheelchair off the mound of snow, he checked the harness. "All set," Sam said gleefully. "Let's do it again."

Daring ran faster with each takeoff, and then lined herself up parallel to the lighthouse until she could drift down for a safer landing.

Sam was beside himself, thrilled beyond words. "You rock, Daring! We're the Crime Fighters, Daring Dog and her partner, Sam the Man!" Sam yelled, his heart beating wildly.

"One more time, girl, before we go home!" Daring wagged her tail joyfully. She had never heard such joy in Sam's voice.

Together, they flew over Misty Harbor, surprising a few neighbors who happened to be outside their homes looking for meteor showers.

Suddenly, Sam saw a flash of silver, and he knew what to do.

"Hang a left Daring." The dog sneezed hard, blinked three times, squinted her eyes, rotated her ears and shifted the position of her tail. They were about to dive in, when Cade saw them.

Cade squinted at the image in the sky. This time he knew he was not imagining things. "You're dead meat" Cade screamed, shaking his fist. "Both of you!"

As Cade ran for his truck, Sam told his Smart Phone to call the police. He disguised his voice so the Chief wouldn't know it was him.

"There's a robbery under way at 52 Schooner Drive. Get there, fast!"

As the police scoured the neighborhood, reports came in about something that looked like a dog and a kid in a weird contraption flying through town. Their phone calls were a source of aggravation for the Chief, who muttered, "Darn, they're about to sell the Lionel trains on the *Home Shopping Network.*" Still, he had a job to do. He scanned the video wall of webcam monitors in the police station. In less than a minute, he could see every major intersection in Misty Harbor. As usual, everything looked quiet and peaceful.

"Earline, everyone knows a dog can't fly," he barked at the town busybody. "Arthur, you need to have your glasses checked," he grumped at the Mayor.

Butters was convinced that the whole town had gone nuts. What was even more incredible was that someone thought there was a kid flying with the dog on some weird contraption. Butters hoisted himself up to check the monitors one more time, zooming in, zooming out, panning right and left. Nada.

Meanwhile, Daring and Sam had returned home, had stashed the sail and harness and were now tucked snugly in bed.

32
Time Heals All Wounds

~

The next day Dr. Trout paid another visit to check on her pets and Daring.

"How y'all doin'?" Archie greeted her as he took her coat.

"Just fine, Archie," she answered. She was wearing a new pair of glasses, and they were not to be missed – shocking pink flamingoes adorned with rhinestone collars perched at either end of leopard skin plastic frames.

Dr. Trout settled down next to Daring and was greeted with warm laps and slurppy kisses. Mackerel dragged his body up, walked over for an ear scratch and settled happily at her feet.

"She's practically good as new," Dr. Trout announced after examining Daring. She smiled at Sam, "She's made a remarkable recovery, Sam, it must be all of the love she's getting in this house."

Sam popped a wheelie and grinned from ear to ear. "Come on, girl, we have to do our homework." Sam and Daring went to his room, closed the door and hit the books. Sam didn't mind doing homework as long as Daring was at his side.

When Dr. Trout put on her thick, down-filled parka ready to leave, she got up her nerve to ask Mr. Harris a very important question. "Do you mind if the rest of the menagerie stays until I set up my new office space?"

Mr. Harris's jaw dropped. He thought Trout had come to fetch her pets.

Seeing him hesitate, Trout sweetened the deal. "Of course you'll have free vet care for Daring for the rest of her life."

Mr. Harris knew he couldn't refuse. "No problem." He was about to ask a question, and then stopped.

Trout arched her brow, squinted hard. "Is there something on your mind?" she asked.

Mr. Harris sighed then asked the question that had been bothering him. "Yes, Dr. Trout – I mean, Hannah Sunshine – do you have any idea how old Daring is?"

"She's probably just a little more than a year old."

Mr. Harris loosened his lariat necktie. "That's a relief, I was just worried that…"

Dr. Trout understood "Don't worry, she's got a long life ahead of her."

"You read my mind. I mean, if she were really old and only had a few more years, I don't know how Sam would handle losing her." Mr. Harris' concern for Sam was certainly understandable.

"Sam's a strong boy," Dr. Trout said softly. "And he's very brave."

Mr. Harris nodded so hard that his hair fell into his eyes. "Let's just say that he can't afford to have his heart broken again."

Dr. Trout shifted her weight and thought about her reply. "You know, Dave, there are no guarantees in life."

"I know, but I can't help but worry," he explained. "I try to insulate him and sometimes I-I-I don't think I'm doing a very good job."

Dr. Trout put her hand on his shoulder. "You have a boy who is able to give love and care to a wounded animal," she said sincerely. "I'd say you are doing a wonderful job."

With a farewell wave, the vet assured him, "You know, there's nothing like a good dog to mend a broken heart."

Mr. Harris nodded. "Yes, that's what I've been thinking, Daring is a real gift to Sam – maybe even an answer to our prayers."

Archie opened the door for the vet. "Bye, y'all," Archie drawled.

"Bye y'all, Archie." Dr. Trout grinned from ear to ear, then raced to her truck. She tooted her horn then clunked down the rocky breakwater road.

Gil and Phil were in good spirits, even when they realized that their mistress had left them behind. Communicating with each other in their own private language, they crossed the room to have their fun.

They walked back and forth in front of Shifty's cage, yawning a loud "meow" to get his attention. When they were sure he was watching them, they batted a toy mouse back and forth because they knew this made him dizzy. Even when Archie said, "Y'all be nice," they kept it up.

As they built up speed, Shifty's head swiveled, left to right, left to right, until – plop, he fell off his perch to land feet up on the bottom of his cage.

33

Button Up and Batten Down

~

The following night Sam scoured the town, clicking on every Misty Harbor webcam to determine where the robber was hiding out. Archie had brought him chocolate pudding to eat at his computer. Sam clicked webcams all over Misty Harbor until he saw a flash of silver coming from a neighborhood on the outskirts of town. Daring perked up. *It's him*, she thought. A low growl began deep in her throat, but it was too dark to see much more.

"Not tonight, Daring. I'm too tired and don't think of going on your own."

Daring heeked half-heartedly. Actually, she was tired, too. Tracking was hard work.

Sam yawned and decided it was time to go to get ready for bed, but before he got very far his Smart Phone text alarm signaled.

LC: U nEd 2 bak ^ Yr hard driV. Storm comin.

SH: Yeah, waves crashing lowd outside

LC: Betcha n skul 2morrow

SH: kewl

LC: wnt me 2 cum Ovr 2morrow?

SH: suR

Archie had been standing in the doorway for a few minutes.. The weather radar on his screen had a flashing red border. A huge, green shape had formed over the Atlantic Ocean. It looked pretty bad.

"Weather alert!" Archie announced. "Y'all pay attention."

"Go tell Dad," Sam said.

Just then, Mr. Harris appeared behind Archie to say goodnight to Sam. "I'm right behind you, Archie, what's going on?"

Archie announced, "A major ocean storm is approaching. Y'all should stoke up the stove. I will conserve power and shut down now." The robot's lights flickered as he walked to his post near the front door. Once he lapsed into sleep mode, his snoring program began to play.

Mr. Harris grabbed his outerwear and raced outside to bring in more firewood. When he finished, he brushed the snow off his coat and hat, and hung them on pegs near the woodstove. Then he got busy stacking the logs and kindling.

"Sam, I'm bringing in extra blankets for you and Daring in case the power goes out and we lose our heat."

"What about the woodstove?" Sam was alarmed. "I thought you said we would never be without heat, Dad. Birds aren't supposed to get cold!"

"I know, Sam. Don't worry, we will use the stove for backup, but I'm saving the wood for as long as I can. I have no idea how much snow we're getting. We could be stuck inside for several days."

"Do you think there'll be school tomorrow?"

"Doubtful, but we won't know until morning."

Gil, Phil, Shifty, and Mackerel had been restless for the previous hour. Animals can sense danger long before humans can. Sam knew that their behavior signaled something big.

"It's a classic Nor'easter," Mr. Harris said as he tucked Sam in for the night. "The buoy report just came in, the waves are already thirty feet high just five miles out," he said, not hiding his concern. "This storm is going to be a doozy."

Mr. Harris kissed his son's forehead and patted Daring's head. Later he climbed the lighthouse stairs to look out at the boiling ocean. Remembering an old photograph that he'd seen in the boathouse, where waves crashed hard against the lighthouse, he ran back inside their snug little house and bolted the doors and windows.

Throughout the night, the wind roared and the waves sprayed higher, sometimes reaching the top of Sam's windows.

Smash! A huge wave slammed against the lighthouse shaking the building so hard that the swing in Shifty's cage rocked back and forth. Daring scampered into bed with Sam. She crawled under the covers, resting her head on Sam's pillow.

"It's okay, girl. You're safe with me," Sam reassured her, pulling her close. Still, Daring trembled.

Shifty squawked frantically, "Hello, Hello, What's up? What's up?" He continued non-stop as the wind rattled the windowpanes and whistled around the lighthouse. Gil and Phil yowled, arched their backs and then pounced onto Sam's bed. Mackerel curled up next to Daring. And finally, they all fell asleep. All except Mr. Harris, that is.

The crackle of the short wave radio had awakened him. It was the Coast Guard announcing a distress call. A Russian fishing boat was in trouble about three miles out at sea. The crew was battling the huge waves that were washing across the bow of their ship. They were taking on so much water that their boat was in danger of sinking. Worse still, their radar was out and no one knew their exact location.

Mr. Harris was glued to his radio as the Coast Guard sent a helicopter to try to find and rescue the crew, but the snow-storm was so fierce, the Coast Guard had to turn back. They would try again at daybreak.

34
Tracking!

~

The next morning, Mr. Harris had to use all of his weight to force the front door open. AND IT WAS STILL SNOWING.

He and Sam ate a hearty breakfast of steaming hot oatmeal, laced with butter and maple syrup. Archie announced, "The temperature is 30 degrees with a wind chill factor of zero degrees. Y'all stay inside."

Daring ran around the room barking to be let out. Mr. Harris opened the door and said, "Be quick, Daring. It's still snowing pretty hard." The local television station announced school cancellations and highway closings. With the weight of the snow building on electrical power wires, the power flickered on and off, prompting Mr. Harris to check the fire in the woodstove.

"ARRRF!" Daring was ready to come in.

Archie opened the door for Daring who was covered with snowflakes from head to tail. With three good shakes, the snowflakes were off Daring and onto the floor.

"Mop the floor, Archie," said Mr. Harris. "Daring, come lie by the stove to warm up." She was there in a wink.

After he poured himself a second cup of coffee, Mr. Harris flicked on the television. The State Police were warning people to stay inside until the storm was over and the roads could be cleared and made safe. There was also an update about the fate of the missing fishing boat. Mr. Harris increased the volume – this was a story of grave concern to everyone.

A Coast Guard spokesperson was being interviewed while standing outside the Coast Guard station where he could barely be heard above the wind. Swirls of thick snowflakes whirled in the background. A helicopter stood ready behind him. "Last night we searched for as long as we could before we had to turn back. The conditions were horrible out there. The waves were at least thirty feet high and the snow was blinding. We're starting a new search right as soon as the wind settles down," he reported.

Daring rotated her ears. She began to drool heavily. *I know what I have to do,* she thought.

"ARRRRRF."

"Again?" Mr. Harris asked the dog.

Whop, whop, whop. Daring made three insistent whops of her tail.

"Archie, open the door."

Archie obeyed and then stood waiting for her to bark to come back in.

Without a second to waste Daring let out a megasneeze, then took off into the storm, flying in a direction she'd never flown before. *Oh my, oh my, oh my – it's bad out here. And cold! But I'm a bloodhound who can track through anything. I'll find them if it's the last thing I do.* She headed straight out to sea, far beyond the lighthouse. Fueled by a harsh wind, snow coated her fur immediately, sticking to it like glue. Daring became a snow-white dog with electric blue feet. She was a funny sight, for sure, but the storm was no laughing matter.

As she flew over the ocean, snow crystals froze on her eyelids. It didn't take very long for her eyes to freeze shut! Now what was she to do? She knew she had to find the boat, but she couldn't open her eyes. *Wait, what was it that the Mrs. Mason taught me? ... Oh, right –Use my nose. It's a magic sniffer.* Daring tried to catch a human scent, but the wind was so strong that any scent disappeared before she could determine its direction. Suddenly, she felt something warm tickle her nose. The sun had broken through the storm clouds and was reflecting off something close to Daring. A golden flash lined up with the sun, and presto! The ice melted off Daring's eyelids. She could open her eyes. *I can see again!*

Now flying at top speed, she spotted the Russian fishing boat. It was being tossed around on the roaring ocean as if it were a toy. And the stern was dangerously low in the water, a sure sign of sinking. The fishermen were huddled together on the deck, holding onto the bow railing. As Daring flew closer, she saw that they were covered in ice from the tips of their heads to their boots.

I'm too late, Daring feared, *they're frozen like blocks of ice.*

Well, it certainly looked that way but when the fishermen saw something in the sky they broke apart and began waving and shouting. They couldn't believe their luck; they were going to be rescued!

But they must have been hallucinating.

Something shaped like a dog was circling their boat. It looked like a white dog with blue feet!!! The fishermen began to cry. "We're imagining things! We've been too cold for too long. We're going to die!"

Too bad I can't talk, Daring thought. *I'll have to find that Coast Guard plane and hope it follows me.*

Daring took a deep breath, let out a big time sneeze then strained her ears. Remarkably, she heard the thump, thump of the Coast Guard helicopter blades above the roar of the wind. She circled away from the boat several times before heading southeast and locating the helicopter.

35
A Bird? A Plane? ... A-A Dog???

~

Coast Guard Lieutenant Christina Martinez was strapped in the pilot's seat. Her co-pilot, Lieutenant Michael Maxwell sat next to her. Together, they searched the ocean for signs of the lost fishing boat. Suddenly, Lt. Maxwell saw Daring through his binoculars.

"Wha - what is *that*?" he gasped.

At the same time, Lt. Martinez spotted Daring. She blinked hard, assumed her eyes were playing tricks on her. *It must be a snow squall,* she thought. Daring's coat was caked with frozen snow and her collar was frozen solid.

"See those blue things?" Lt. Maxwell asked Lt. Martinez, who was blinking harder, trying to focus on what she knew couldn't be real.

"IS THAT A BIRD???" she asked, shocked at the size of the thing.

Daring swooped into position, flying alongside the pilot's window. When she opened her mouth to bark, a large glob of drool flew out and froze instantly. She looked like she had silver wires coming out of her mouth. Lt. Martinez turned the helicopter sharply, away from the weird looking bird flying next to her, but she couldn't escape Daring.

Taking a great risk of being sliced up by the helicopter blades, Daring landed on the helicopter pontoons. She pressed her face against the pilot's window and barked her wonderfully weird, baying, moan.

"It's attacking us!" Lt. Maxwell cried as Daring bayed and barked. She just wanted them to follow her. *What's wrong with them?* she wondered. Trying another tactic, Daring pushed off from the helicopter, and pointed her left paw in the direction of the fishing boat. When Lt. Martinez didn't follow her, Daring repeated her effort two more times, until finally it dawned on the pilot.

"I think it wants us to follow it,"Lt. Martinez said, turning toward Daring. Although the copilot was skeptical, he agreed. A few minutes later Daring lead the helicopter to the fishing boat, leaving the amazed pilots to rescue the grateful Russians.

"I'll be darned!" Lt. Martinez said, spotting the boat. "Radio it in and then let's pick 'em up!"

Just as they pulled the last fisherman into the helicopter, the storm gained strength. The helicopter dipped once toward the sinking boat then headed back to Misty Harbor. Daring was about to leave, too, until she heard a sound above the roar of the storm. Circling back above the boat, Daring could see where the sound was coming from. There was a small dog huddled under a bench in front of the wheelhouse. Vronsky, a little brown, black and white mutt, who belonged to the ship's captain, had been left behind in all the confusion.

Daring swooped down, landed on the deck of the sinking boat, and then tried to squeeze her large body under the bench where the frightened dog was hiding. Try as she might, Daring wouldn't fit, but her paws could reach the dog. With a few gentle touches, Daring coaxed him out.

As the boat rocked and rolled in the huge waves, Vronsky was terrified, crying and shivering violently. *Poor baby,* Daring thought. With three warm, tender laps, Daring calmed the dog long enough to pick it up by the scruff of its neck. With Vronsky's little feet dangling above the deck, the surprised but grateful dog was carried off in the safety of Daring's mouth.

Back in Misty Harbor, Daring dropped Vronsky in front of the Coast Guard station where the helicopter had landed a few minutes earlier. The little dog barked furiously until someone opened the door.

"Vronsky!" the Russian Captain cried when he saw his dog. "How did you get here?" The captain was incredulous. Surely she didn't swim. He turned to his crew. "Did one of you bring Vronsky?"

To a man, they shook their heads in denial.

"Then truly this is a miracle!" The Captain and his crew lifted their eyes to the sky, but all they could see was a white blob with flashes of electric blue. In a blink, the vision disappeared.

Freezing cold and in need of her warm bed, an exhausted Daring finally returned home. Archie scolded her when she barked at the door, "Gad bawg".

Sam had been crying, afraid that Daring had been blown into the ocean and that he'd lost her forever. When he saw his now white dog standing in front of him, he threw his arms around her neck. "Don't ever do that again," he sobbed. Daring gave him a look that said it all. *I was being a bloodhound, Sam. I was tracking!*

That night, the television news reporter's interview with Lt. Martinez was the top feature.

"It was the strangest thing we'd ever seen," Lt. Martinez remarked. "It was the size of a large dog, but it was all white and weird as this sounds – it had blue feet."

"Oh, really?" Sam said slyly, "So that's where you've been." Sam gave Daring a playful nudge. He hugged her and said, "You *tracked* them – AMAZING! You're the best bloodhound in the world. And you're mine!"

As Daring warmed up, the snow caking her coat melted, leaving big puddles on the floor. Archie mopped them up while Mr. Harris used towel after towel to dry her off. He hadn't heard the television news, which was just as well. For now, Daring's special talents were a secret between Sam and herself. And that was the way they wanted to keep it. Early the next morning, Sam was finally able to remove the blue paint from Daring's feet using a safe, homemade concoction he'd located on the internet.

36
Loose Lips Sink Ships

~

By the following morning, the storm was over. Roads were plowed and salted and the town was back to normal. At The Seafarer's Diner, Sgt. Copper and Sgt. Beech were wolfing down a blueberry pancake breakfast. Cade was there, as well, stuffing his face with huge amounts of food from the buffet. The policemen were discussing the events of the past week.

"First, there were the reports of the flying dog and the kid," Beech said as he drizzled some extra maple syrup on his pancakes. "Then, there was the Coast Guard report about the white animal with blue feet that led them to the sinking trawler," he continued, shaking his head in disbelief.

"And if that wasn't enough, no one could explain how the little Russian dog showed up at the door of the Coast Guard Station," Sgt. Copper added.

"Something very strange is going on," Copper said to Beech.

Sgt. Copper took a swig of his coffee then continued. "You know, one of the people who called in – a real nut – said the kid looked like Sam Harris."

Cade's ears twitched. Did he hear right? He draped his arm casually over the back of the seat and turned to the policemen.

"Excuse me," Cade said, a polite phrase he rarely used. "I heard about that, too. Who's this kid, Sam Harris?"

"Oh, that's the lighthouse keeper's kid," Beech answered.

Cade smiled. He'd passed the breakwater leading to the lighthouse dozens of times. *Maybe I'm about to get lucky.*

"Does he have a dog?" Cade asked, his tongue flicking in and out like the snake that he is.

"Yeah, he just got a mutt. Hideous looking creature," Copper laughed.

Cade begins to drool in his excitement. "Is it brown?"

"Color of baby poop," Copper laughed again.

"It wouldn't be a bloodhound, would it?"

"Could be," Beech answered.

A wicked smile crossed Cade's face. *Oh, Daring. You are going to fetch a very tidy sum,"* he thought, letting out a long burp as he put on his hat and slinked out the door.

37
The Holiday Spirit
~

M r. Harris and Archie were busy loading the car with new computer equipment for the school. Working with a bunch of his old computer parts, he had built an amazing communications station to replace the school's stolen computers. Sam had to admit it was extremely cool of his dad. So cool that he ignored his father's croadeling, for the moment.

Sam stayed home to do his homework while Mr. Harris spent a few hours setting up a computer station in the library. It was state-of-the-art, with wireless access all over the school. When Mr. Harris returned, he and Sam ate a hearty fish chowder and a big salad that Archie had prepared earlier in the day. Then they proceeded to get ready for the holiday program that night at Sam's school.

After a nice hot shower, Mr. Harris stood in front of the mirror shaving. All of a sudden, what looked like a shower of golden dust appeared. When he put his glasses on to see it better, the dusty glow had disappeared. "I've been seeing things lately," he muttered to himself. Mr. Harris blinked several times, shrugged his shoulders, and then went back to his shaving.

The school auditorium was filled with parents and kids excited to hear the performance of *Peter and the Wolf.* By the time Sam and his father arrived, the orchestra kids' families were already in their seats. Many of the Crabs were there, too, dragged along by their parents. Basil was slouched in a chair next to his father. They were sitting directly in front of the Harrises.

The evening began with an announcement from the principal, whose name was Mr. Duncan Duncan. The short, barrel-bellied man had one long strand of black hair on his head. It was plastered with goo from left to right and looked like someone had taken a pen and drawn a line over his bald head.

Mr. Duncan Duncan adjusted the microphone, and then cleared his throat. "We want to begin by thanking Mr. Davidson Harris for his very generous donation to the school," he began. "Mr. Harris has installed a computer kiosk in our library where our students can have access to powerful web browsers."

"Oooh," the crowd murmured. Mr. Duncan continued, "These browsers will allow our students to get any information that they need to help them do their homework."

Parents applauded, while a muffled groan from the Crabs filled the auditorium.

Mr. Duncan cleared his throat again. "Mr. Harris also tells me that he's programmed the computer to allow students to listen to music and play games! But first..."

A loud cheer filled the auditorium. "Ayuh! But *first* they will need to log in and take a short test on current events," Mr. Duncan said with a chuckle.

The Crabs groaned and moaned.

"And Mr. Harris has also rigged up the computer kiosk with satellite access and a direct link to the Hubbell telescope so you can see what the Hubble is seeing ... when it is seeing it!"

The audience whistled and cheered, all except the Crabs, of course. They were so intent on hating school that they couldn't imagine what this meant.

Mr. Duncan looked in the direction of Mr. Harris. "Dave, this is incredibly generous of you, truly amazing! Ayuh! Thank you so much! And I understand that your son Sam helped you put this together," he said, pumping his fist in celebration. "A special thank you goes to our student, Sam Harris."

As the applause began, Sam slinked down in his wheel-chair. He was so embarrassed he wanted to disappear.

Basil turned around to look at Sam.

"Hey," he said.

"What do you want?" Sam mumbled.

"I just want to say that –"

Suddenly, everyone was laughing.

Daring had somehow gotten into the auditorium and was lumbering across the stage. She sneezed hard when she reached the podium, slinging some snot in Mr. Duncan's direction. While the audience cracked up, Daring scanned the room. Bingo! She waddled down the stage stairs, and then plopped in front of Sam's wheelchair.

"Quiet," Mr. Duncan said into the microphone. Then he nodded to the music teacher. Tap, tap, and tap. Mr. Figaro tapped his baton. The crowd settled down.

The audience applauded as the kids in the orchestra picked up their instruments. Lily spotted Sam in the audi-ence. She mouthed a hello. After a few seconds of screech-ing violins being tuned and clarinet reeds squeaking, the orchestra was ready.

The music began. *Toodle-oodle-doo-dee-doo-dee-doooooo.*

Then, much to Sam's horror, Mr. Harris began humming off key along with the orchestra! Basil's shoulders shook with laughter. Seeing this, Sam wanted to die!

Mr. Harris finally stifled himself when he saw Sam slouch down in his seat and Daring cover her ears.

"Sorry, Sam," he said quietly, "I didn't mean to embarrass you." Then Mr. Harris leaned to whisper to Basil! "If you think that's funny, come by some time and hear me yodel."

Just as Sam was about to explode at his father's obvious attempt to forge a friendship for him, Basil turned and smiled at Sam. "Maybe I will, if it's okay with Sam."

What?!? Sam was certain that Basil had been dropped on his head.

Mr. Harris turned to his son. "Well, Sam?"

"Sure," Sam mumbled with more enthusiasm than he meant to show.

It was Lily's shining hour. She played her tuba better than she'd ever played before. Although she missed a couple of notes and gave out one nail-across-the-blackboard squeak, to Sam and the rest of the audience, she was perfection.

After the concert, Lily's mom invited Sam and Mr. Harris back to her house for apple pan dowdy and ice cream. Mr. Harris straightened his lariat and licked his lips; a short "yodel-lay-ti" escaped his throat.

Lily's mom laughed. "I'm not sure it's that good."

38
Lost and Found

~

That weekend, as Sam and Lily were in his room putting the final touches on their movie, Daring looked out the window and saw what appeared to be paw prints in the snow. She raced to the door, barking and sneezing. Archie opened the door to let her out, then returned to finish his chores. Sneezing and bouncing her way through the snow, Daring followed the tracks. Sam logged on to Daring's webcam so he and Lily could follow her.

Daring stopped at the boathouse, scrunched down, and heeked. When she moved closer, a tiny brown nose poked out from under a tarp.

"It's Prince Charming!" Lily said amazed.

"Quick, go get him!" Sam told Lily. She raced out the door and then crept up quietly to the boathouse. "Good girl, Daring, you found Prince Charming."

Lily bent down slowly, then held out her palm so the cat could see that she was friendly. Then, ever so carefully, Lily reached in and pulled the shivering cat into her arms. She snuggled the cat against her chest and then ran back to the house, a proud Daring close behind.

"There you go, kitty, kitty," she cooed as she stroked the poor Siamese cat. "Time to go home to mama," she whispered, patting the cat's snow-covered fur as Gil and Phil watched warily from their beds in front of the woodstove.

"Great tracking, Daring," Sam said, praising his dog for being such a good bloodhound.

"Dood gawg," Archie chimed in.

This is what it feels like to be a good bloodhound, Daring realized. *I feel great!* Daring moved close to the shivering cat, guarding her find.

"Should we call Mrs. Grady, or just take her the cat?" Lily asked, so excited and eager to share the good news.

"Why don't you call her first and then I'll take you," Mr. Harris offered.

"No, we can do it," Sam answered. "Lily, how about I hold the cat, you push my wheelchair and we go straight to her house?"

"Sure, let's do it," Lily agreed, and then she paused. "I'm not that strong, though and it's kinda far," she worried.

"The sidewalks are shoveled and my chair moves pretty fast. Mrs. Grady lives only a block away," Sam argued.

"Hold on for a minute, kids," Mr. Harris said. He returned in a minute with a pillowcase and handed it to Sam.

"Put Prince Charming in the pillowcase so he doesn't get loose again."

Sam and Lily looked at Mr. Harris and realized he was right. It would be a tragedy to have found the cat, only to lose him before getting him to his owner.

Lily huffed and puffed as she pushed Sam's wheelchair, and was almost out of breath when they reached Mrs. Grady's front door.

"Made it," Lily said excitedly, as she took Prince Charming from the pillowcase, and then rang Mrs. Grady's doorbell.

Mrs. Grady opened the door part way, and peered out. "Who's there?" she asked in a shaky voice.

"It's Prince Charming!" Lily shouted.

Mrs. Grady threw open the door in time for Prince Charming to leap from Lily's arms and run into the house.

"Where have you been, naughty boy?" Mrs. Grady asked her cat. Then Mrs. Grady looked incredulously at Sam and Lily.

"Thank you from the bottom of my heart!" she blurted, fighting back joyful tears. "You children are going to get a very handsome reward," she promised.

"We didn't do it, Mrs. Grady," Sam said. "It was my dog who really found her."

"Well, I'm going to have to bake her some biscuits," Mrs. Grady said as she waved goodbye to the kids.

When they returned to the lighthouse, Sam wheeled himself to his computer and pulled up the video file. To the last frame, he added, "Case Solved!"

39
Revenge
~

In Misty Harbor, life settled down for a few quiet days, or so it seemed. School vacation had begun and everyone was busy doing pre-holiday errands and chores. Daring was content to patrol around the lighthouse sniffing and sneezing, trying to get her nose in shape for her next adventure.

Sam was busy working on a software program that would send signals to his Smart Phone whenever a robbery was reported in Misty Harbor. Mr. Harris was spending a lot of time in the boathouse putting the finishing touches on the catboat. Unfortunately, they were both so focused on their projects that they didn't see Cade parked at the end of the breakwater.

Cleverly, Cade had brought slices of roast beef with him to tempt Daring to come close enough so he could grab her. He sat patiently in his truck, waiting to make his move.

As the day progressed, Archie was inside the house vacuuming the rugs while a turkey was roasting in the oven. Meanwhile, Sam had tested his new software and satisfied that it would work, he needed a break. He pulled on his winter hat and jacket, then wheeled himself outside behind the lighthouse to get a little fresh air and to call Lily. As they chatted, Sam took a moment to reach into one of the storage baskets attached to his wheelchair. He put Lily on speaker and began focusing his binoculars. Sam had learned to expect the unexpected when living next to the ocean.

"After that big storm a few days ago, you'd think there'd be whitecaps or something," he said, "the water's really calm."

"Mom says it's like nature's way of catching her breath," Lily explained.

Sam pressed his binoculars to his eyes and slowly searched the ocean surface. When he saw some sudden movement, he zoomed in for a closer look.

"Wow, there's a pod of dolphins right near me," he exclaimed.

"Show me," Lily asked. Sam slid the camera function on this Smart Phone to FaceTime, and aimed it toward the pod.

"Wicked cool," he could hear her exclaim, "you are so lucky to live out there."

Sam didn't answer. He still would prefer to be back in his old house in Massachusetts.

When he reversed the phone's direction, Lily could see Cade holding the roast beef out for Daring.

"Who's that guy?" she asked.

"What guy?"

"The one who just picked up Daring." Lily said. Her instincts told her something was wrong.

Sam spun around in time to see Cade snatch Daring and run with her to the truck. Sam's heart was beating so hard in his chest that he could feel it pounding in his head. He screamed, "Dad, DAD, call the police – he took Daring!!!"

Mr. Harris ran outside with the portable phone to his ear and tried to stay calm, while getting information from Sam to give to Chief Butters. After wheeling Sam back inside the house, Mr. Harris began pacing back and forth. "This can't be happening," he worried, wringing his hands. "It can't, I won't let it!" Mr. Harris began pulling at his hair in frustration.

Sam sat stonily in his wheelchair; he began to tremble.

"WELLBEENER Alert," warned Archie.

Mr. Harris ran to Sam and waved his WELLBEENER over his son. Sam's pulse was racing off the charts.

"Take a deep breath," his father said shakily. Sam ignored him.

Mr. Harris put his arms around his son and ignored Sam's futile struggle to break loose.

"You have to breathe slowly and calm yourself down," Mr. Harris begged, worried that his worst fears were coming true. "We will find your dog and bring her home, Sam. They couldn't have gone very far."

Sgt. Copper and Sgt. Beech arrived in record time, but all they could get out of Sam was that he thought it was the same man who'd been breaking into houses.

Moments later, Lily arrived. She was barely able to catch her breath. "I ran all the way once I saw what happened!"

"Wait, a minute – you *saw* it happen?" Mr. Harris was incredulous. "How?"

"We were live chatting and I could see it happening behind Sam."

Mr. Harris ran into Sam's room. Sam was staring out his bedroom window, praying for Daring to return.

"Give me your phone, Sam. I might be able to capture the image that Lily saw."

"Leave me alone, please," Sam murmured flatly. "She's gone, Dad. She's gone."

I should have known she was too good to be true, Sam thought.

"Listen to me, Sam," his father was adamant. "I promise you that I will turn this town upside down until I find your dog and bring her home. You just have to have faith in me."

Sam tossed the phone and his father grabbed it. Mr. Harris ran to his workshop and plugged Sam's phone into his computer. Then he opened a software program that he'd written that would allow him to tap into the phone's memory and – presto! He had a very clear image of Cade with the struggling Daring in his arms.

While Copper and Beech were reviewing the footage on Sam's phone, Dr. Fanny Sunshine Trout appeared at the door.

"Your father called me, Sam. I'm here to help," she announced.

Copper studied the video clip. "Whoa, that's the same fella that asked us about Sam when we were in the diner this morning," he told Beech.

"You *know* him?" Mr. Harris exclaimed hopefully.

"Wouldn't say we know him, but we sure did speak to him and I think he got into a silver pickup when he left."

Sgt. Beech headed for the door. "I'll do an All Points Bulletin for a silver truck with a man and dog in it right now."

"Thank you, Sergeant. Please, you have no idea what this dog means to my boy – er, to this family," Mr. Harris said, fighting back tears. "You have to get her back for us, please."

"Please," Shifty said from his cage.

"Please," Archie said.

Burp, went Mackerel, while Gil and Phil watched from a windowsill.

⌒◦

The house was a beehive of activity as word went out about Daring. The local television station announced the All Points Bulletin and gave instructions on what to do if anyone saw the getaway truck with a man and a bloodhound in the cab.

Although Lily and Dr. Trout tried to comfort Sam, their efforts were in vain. The more they talked to him, the quieter he became until finally he couldn't take it.

"Leave me alone!" he pleaded, before burying his face in his hands and sobbing uncontrollably.

"Lily, please give us a moment," Dr. Trout said while handing a tissue to Lily, who'd begun to cry.

"Thanks," Lily said and she went to sit in the living room.

Dr. Trout pulled up a chair beside Sam.

"Listen to me, Sam, please hear what I say," Dr. Trout said, her face directly in front of Sam's. "Did you ever hear anyone say 'It's always the darkest before the dawn'?" Sam shook his head 'no', he had never heard anyone say that.

"She'll be back, Sam. You just wait and see."

"No she won't. *You* wait and see." Sam had learned that lesson at an early age.

"Tish, tish, tish. This is really, really, really troubling, Sam," she said, pulling up a chair next to him. "You are sad and scared and I am too, but I know something you don't know about Daring and now I'm going to tell you," she continued.

Sam couldn't help but be interested. So with one eye watching the window as the sun dropped beneath the horizon, Sam turned to listen to Dr. Fanny Sunshine Trout.

The good doctor spoke in barely a whisper, causing Sam to wheel himself closer to her. "This is between you and me – and Grouper, okay?"

"Okay," he mumbled.

Sam studied the vet's face. Her eyes were so kind, her expression so gentle, so caring. She almost reminded Sam of his mother. Unable to hold in his feelings, puddles of tears spilled from his eyes.

Swiftly, Dr. Trout produced a tissue from the sleeve of her sweater. She offered it to Sam who didn't take it. Instead, he took her hand and squeezed it so tight that the good veterinarian choked back a sob.

"When we were operating on her ..." she began, "At first, Grouper and I paid no attention to it. We were both concentrating so hard on saving her life. But we both felt it, sure as I'm here with you right now..." The story of the puffs of golden dust, the unexplained warm breeze that entered the room, kept Sam mesmerized.

It took Dr. Trout fifteen minutes to tell the entire story of the operation to save his dog. "She's magical, Sam, you have to believe it – somehow Daring will find her way back to you. I am sure of it."

Should Sam believe her? After all, Daring could fly and that certainly took some magical power. *But my mom had magical powers too.* Sam reasoned. *She could communicate with whales without saying a word and look what happened to her! No, Daring is gone for good. I just wish I had never met her.*

40
A Load Off His Shoulders

~

At eleven p.m. the search for Daring was called off for the night. Exhausted and filled with fear, Sam reluctantly got into bed, closed his eyes and fell into a troubled sleep.

BLUE! It's so dark out, I'm shivering. Mommy, where are you? What happened? I'm so confused. I feel you underneath me. You're right there. Say something, Mom. TALK TO ME. PLEASE, MOM, PLEASE. YOU PROMISED! MOM! NO, NO, NO!

Mr. Harris was out of bed and into Sam's room as quickly as he could. "Sam, Sam – oh my poor son, wake up, please – you're having a bad, bad dream!" Sam was trembling violently when he opened his eyes, but when his father reached out to hold him, he pushed him away.

"Get out!" Sam screamed. "Leave me alone! And get that WELLBEENER away from me."

Mr. Harris rose from Sam's bed, but instead of doing as Sam demanded, he pulled up a chair. He took a deep breath and somehow found the strength to be firm with the boy whom he had coddled ever since the accident.

"We are doing everything we can to find her, Sam," he began. "The police have had several tips come in and they are following up on them. You just have to be patient and pray that this will be over in the morning."

"Whatever you say, Dad, you're always right," Sam barked.

Unfazed by his son's predictable reaction, Mr. Harris continued, "I really believe she'll be found and returned to us, Sam. I want you to have a little confidence in me."

"Why should I?" Sam reached under his pillow for his mother's hat and began rubbing it against his cheek.

"Be-be-because I'm your father and I love you more than life itself," Mr. Harris blurted.

"Can't you see what's happening, Dad? You live in your dream world with your computers and inventions and everything you do – and you have a life! I don't. I hate my life. I hate my wheelchair. I hate my school and the ONLY reason I can feel happy is because of Daring. And now she's gone."

"And we'll get her back, Sam, give me a chance."

"Reality, Dad. I'm bad luck." Sam felt cold, he shivered and it was hard for him to breath.

"Don't say that, Sam."

"It's true. If I hadn't told Mom I was bored, maybe we wouldn't have been on that glacier." Finally, he was opening up.

Mr. Harris shook his head in disagreement and allowed a slight smile to cross his lips. "Sam, your mother was a very careful person. No one – not even you – could convince her to do something she didn't think was right."

"You weren't there, Dad," Sam argued, "You didn't see where we went."

"No, I wasn't there, but there *were* others who were. You can't believe that you convinced a whole team of scientists to put their safety in danger."

Sam was quiet for a moment, and then blurted, "Maybe she wouldn't have given in to me if I hadn't thrown a fit ..."

Mr. Harris studied his son. The troubled young boy looked like he was about to explode. His face was beet red, his hands trembling. *Now's the time,* Mr. Harris realized. Finally.

"Do you remember where you were when it happened?" Mr. Harris asked quietly.

"Sort of," Sam answered, surprising his father.

"Will you tell me about it?" Mr. Harris said, almost in a whisper.

Sam settled back on his pillows.

"It was really sunny, pretty warm out. I even took my jacket off when the helicopter let us out."

"Did you land on the glacier?"

"Yeah. It was really cool flying up there. We saw these strange goats with curly horns and some other animals," Sam said. He looked off in the distance as he unlocked his painful memories.

"So you were having a special time, right Sam? Wasn't that your first ride in a helicopter?"

Sam nodded, "I just remember it was hot out and Mom was afraid that the ice would be melting and it would be dangerous. But I begged her because she had promised we'd do our first hike on a glacier together."

"And Mom kept her promises," his father reminded him.

"Yes." Sam had stopped crying and could speak more clearly.

"So then what happened?" Mr. Harris asked, prying gently.

"So we started across the glacier and the guide had an ice axe so he went first. Mom was roped to me. The others weren't."

Mr. Harris could imagine Louise carefully roping herself to their son.

The expression on Sam's face changed as he sat silently for a moment. Then he whispered, "I can hear the sound sometimes."

"What sound?" his father asked.

"Pick, pick, step. Pick, pick step," Sam said. "You put the ice axe in twice, then you take a step."

Sam closed his eyes and allowed himself to remember the moment he had tried so hard to forget – the nightmare that followed *pick, pick step.*

"Then there was a crack. And Mom screamed and I was flying down on top of her, down deep into the crevasse. The ice was blue – deep blue. And maybe I hit my head or something, but I knew I was on top of Mom but she wouldn't speak to me. And it was cold, Dad, and I was shivering and men were yelling to me not to move, so I told Mom not to move BUT SHE DIDN'T ANSWER ME."

Mr. Harris pulled a quilt over Sam's trembling body, thinking the boy had said enough, but Sam continued. He *had* to tell his story, had to let it out and then take his punishment – as if there was anything else bad that could happen to him.

"Someone grabbed me. I think it was the pilot, but I'm not sure. And they pulled me out first. And then Mom."

Mr. Harris knew how dangerous it had been for the rescuers. He knew there was extreme bravery and that a member of the team was lowered into the crevasse to pull out his wife and son.

"And I thank God that they saved you," his father said, wiping away his own tears.

"But not Mom, she was hurt too bad."

"Yes, I-I know, son."

"She tried to stay alive – she promised." Sam was crying, barely able to speak.

"Sam, she was unconscious, she couldn't have –"

"You're wrong," Sam shook his head forlornly. "Mom was still breathing when they got her up and when she was lying on the ice next to me, I begged her, Dad, I begged her not to die."

"Oh, Sam – she was gravely injured," Mr. Harris reminded him, while choking back his own tears.

"You know what she said to me?" Sam lowered his head, unable to look at his father.

"She spoke?" Mr. Harris was stunned. This was the first he had heard of Louise being conscious after the accident. "Tell me," he whispered, his tears flowing freely.

"Mom looked right at me and said 'I'm not going to die, Sam – I promise'. And then – and then she said 'I love you and your daddy' and she closed her eyes and faced the sun. And they put me on a stretcher, but not her, Dad. She died right there – right after she promised she wouldn't."

Sam took a few deep breaths and for the first time since he was a small boy, he allowed his father to rock him in his arms as sobs tore from his body.

"It was not your fault, Sam, you have to forgive yourself. Your mom wanted to share her life with you, her experiences, her knowledge and her passions. You must understand that trip was as much for her as it was for you. She loved hiking on glaciers almost as much as she liked studying whales – and Sam, she knew the danger, especially in the summer when ice melts."

"I know, but Dad –"

"Shhh. Let me finish. As spectacular as your mom was, she was only human. And humans make mistakes. It was a mistake to hike on a glacier when ice was melting. Even the most experienced guides in the world have fallen into crevasses and many of them have not lived to tell about it. If I know your mother, she was torn between having the experience of crossing that glacier – she'd talked about it for months – and being overly cautious. After all, she had her most precious possession in the world with her – you."

"You think?" Sam looked deeply into his father's eyes.

"I *know*, son. I'm sure." *That was it,* Mr. Harris prayed. *The hurt, the pain and the guilt living inside his son had finally escaped.*

Mr. Harris settled Sam back down on his pillows. "Say your prayers, Sam, for your mom and for Daring – and maybe even for me, if you want. Now go to sleep."

Mr. Harris waited the few minutes it took for Sam to fall back to sleep. Then he climbed the stairs to the lighthouse very slowly, until he reached the top.

"Louise, Louise," he said, holding her image in his mind. He saw it so clearly now, a terrible accident, a child riddled with guilt, a devoted mother giving her last message of love. Their son had been through too much, both legs were broken in the fall, he'd endured endless surgeries and doctors could not explain why the boy still couldn't feel anything. And now, when there was a glimmer of hope for his recovery, the one thing he had allowed himself to care about since the accident was taken from him.

"It's just not fair, Louise, Just not fair."

41

The Miracle of the Light

~

Three days passed without any success in finding Cade and Daring. It was the first night of Hanukah and Archie's hologram featured a menorah with the first candle being lit. A holiday song, "Dreidel, Dreidel, Dreidel," played repeatedly. Lily insisted that Sam and his father come to her house for a traditional lighting of the menorah and delicious roast brisket and potato latkes. "I won't take no for an answer," she announced to Sam.

"Nor will I," said Mr. Harris.

And so the Harrises and the Cohens celebrated the holiday – the Festival of Lights. After saying prayers and lighting the first candle, Lily told the story of Hanukah – the miracle of the light.

"There was only enough oil in the great synagogue for the candelabra to give light for one day – instead it lasted for eight days. It was a miracle, Sam."

Sam just smiled. *If Lily wants to believe in miracles, that's up to her. I know better,* he thought.

Mr. Harris spent the following day putting up their Christmas tree. Sam sat somberly in his wheelchair, squeezing Daring's ball between his fingers. The dog had been gone for nearly a week and Sam had pretty much given up on ever seeing her again. Throughout the day, there were visitors. Sgt. Copper and Sgt. Beech came by often to reassure Sam that they were still following leads. Dr. Trout dropped off a basket of treats for the Harrises and her pets who remained with the Harrises while her home was under repair – and right before dinner a group of people stood in front of the lighthouse singing Christmas carols, as fluffy snowflakes drifted to the ground. Although their music was beautiful and joyous, it hit a sour note with Sam, who could only worry if Daring was being cared for.

Meanwhile, Basil and his father were on their way out of Misty Harbor to a tree farm where they could cut their own Christmas tree. The frigid air stung; it was so cold that Mr. Pettibone suggested that they just buy one of the pre-cut trees. "It's freezing out – too cold to be tramping around out in the woods," he apologized, knowing that Basil loved doing the sawing with him.

"I couldn't care less," Basil answered moodily. He meant it. Ever since his parents' divorce, holidays had not been the happiest times. Both his mother and father fought over whom he could be with and when, yet they didn't pay much attention to him once they'd won their argument.

Mr. Pettibone chose a six-foot tree that would fit nicely in his living room. "Help me tie this onto the roof, Basil," he asked while struggling with the tree, "it's a two-person job."

With lackluster energy, Basil slid out of the car and was about to join his father when he noticed a silver truck matching the description of the one on the news.

"Dad," he whispered. "That looks like the truck that they showed on TV, the guy that stole the dog."

Mr. Pettibone rested their tree against the car trunk so he could get a better look.

"You might be right," Mr. Pettibone whispered.

"Let's see if there's a dog inside," Basil said.

His father agreed and they hurried to the truck. Just as they reached the passenger door and were about to peer in, Cade came flying out of nowhere.

"HEY! GET AWAY FROM MY TRUCK!" he yelled.

Cade, who'd been out to buy a tree of his own, ran toward them, but not in time to stop Daring from sitting up and looking out the window.

"That's Daring! You stole that dog!" Basil screamed as Cade reached his truck. Quickly, Mr. Pettibone dialed 9-1-1 and gave their location and information.

"STOP HIM! Basil shouted to the customers in line to pay for their trees. "He stole that dog!"

As some customers ran to help, Cade jumped inside his truck and fumbled with his keys, trying to find the ignition. People were banging on his window.

Sensing freedom, Daring gave a quick jerk to the old rope he had tied her with – and SNAP!

Cade was unprepared for the new Daring Dog. She turned on him quickly, her teeth flashing, drool gushing. Daring threw her weight against him, biting his leg first and then his hand, while pinning him against the door.

"Let go of me, you filthy mutt," Cade hollered as Daring took another bite of his leg.

"My leg, my leg," Cade howled as sirens screamed in the distance.

"Open the passenger door," someone yelled, and Mr. Pettibone did just that.

Daring leaped out of the truck and covered Basil with kisses and slobber!

Even though he thought it was gross, Basil didn't really care. What was more important was the warm feeling that came over him, knowing what finding Daring will mean to his classmate – the boy whom he had made very miserable in the past.

"Come on, Daring," said Basil, as he patted the excited dog "we'll take you home, girl."

"Not so fast," said Sgt. Copper, followed by Sgt. Beech who had just handcuffed Cade.

"What's the problem, officer?" asked Mr. Pettibone.

Sgt. Copper took a photo of Daring out of his wallet and held it up next to Daring's face. "I need to make a positive identification first." Copper squinted at the dog, and then shook his head.

"Satisfied?" Mr. Pettibone asked.

"Satisfied," Copper said. "Okay, Daring," he said, "Let's go home."

Basil stepped forward. "I'd like to do that, if that's okay with you."

Mr. Pettibone shook his head and turned to Sgt. Copper. "She belongs to my son's schoolmate and they've had kind of a rough beginning."

Copper scratched his chin. "How about if you take her and we follow?"

"That's a deal," Basil said. "Come on girl, let's go see Sam!"

Sam, my buddy, my best friend, I've been so worried about him. I can't believe it, I'm going to see Sam. I'm going HOME! With that, Daring leaped into the back seat of Mr. Pettibone's car for the short trip to the Harrises.

In their haste to leave, the Pettibones' tree was left in the parking lot.

42
The Greatest Gift
~

At the Harris home, despite his father's attempt at holiday cheer, the mood was gloomy. Sam could care less about the holidays. "What's there to celebrate?" he'd asked his father earlier at dinner. He'd lost his appetite and just pushed his uneaten food around his plate.

"Aren't you feeling well?" Mr. Harris asked, "Let me take your temperature." He moved closer to Sam and started to wave the WELLBEENER over him.

"I'M FINE," Sam shouted, "Get that thing away from me!"

Mr. Harris turned away. There was no dealing with his son who was mourning the loss of his dog.

"Y'all have a choice of chocolate or strawberry ice cream," Archie announced.

"I'll have strawberry, Archie. Sam, what will you have?" his father asked.

Sam sat silently.

"Y'all want hot cocoa?" Archie asked.

Sam didn't answer at first, then mumbled "Okay".

"Y'all want farshmella muff?" Archie garbled.

"It's Marshmallow FLUFF, you dumb robot," Sam growled.

"Sam, please!" his father begged, "let's try not to completely spoil the evening."

Mr. Harris had spent the better part of the afternoon decorating their tree and stringing lights. He had done his best to create a festive atmosphere in their home, although there was nothing he could do to cheer up his son.

"Archie, please choose a selection of Christmas music to play while I light up the tree."

Immediately, the sounds of, "Rudolph the Red-Nosed Reindeer," filled the room. Shifty sang along, choosing to sing only the word "nose", but knowing exactly when to sing it.

Mr. Harris was standing back admiring the tree when he saw a flashing blue light coming down the breakwater. "Police approaching," Archie announced.

Oh no, Mr. Harris thought. *If it were good news, they would have called.*

Sam saw the blue lights, too. He couldn't bear what he thought he was about to hear so he wheeled himself into his room. He put his ear pods in and turned up the volume. *I'll just close my eyes, crank the music and zone out,* he thought.

The moment the Pettibones stepped out of the car, Daring bolted to Sam's window and stood there heeking. Into his zone and with his eyes shut tightly, Sam heard nothing.

With his proud father standing beside him, Basil knocked on the front door.

Mr. Harris's hands were trembling as he answered the door. He didn't expect to see Basil and his father standing there. A strange feeling passed over him. It made no sense that a warm breeze was tickling his cheek on this cold December night. From behind the Pettibones, he could see a parade of police cars and their flashing blue lights. Then it appeared that there were people running down the breakwater cheering and a news helicopter flying overhead.

"May I help you?" he asked solemnly, bracing himself for bad news.

"I found Sam's dog!" Basil announced, a huge smile stretching from ear to ear.

"What did you say?" Mr. Harris leaned closer to Basil as the sound of the helicopter was making it hard for him to hear.

Just then, Daring raced to the door, sprinted by Mr. Harris and Archie and sped around the living room looking for Sam, whose door remained closed.

"Come in, come in," Mr. Harris beckoned, his heart soaring with joy. He pointed out the door to Sam's room. "He's in there, why don't you deliver the good news."

Basil knocked on Sam's door just as a song ended on his iPod. Sam heard the knock, wheeled himself to the door, but didn't open it.

"Just say it," he muttered from inside his room, knowing for sure that his dog was dead.

"It's me, Basil. I found your dog! Open the door!!!"

I must be dreaming, Sam thought. *I thought I heard Basil say he found my dog.*

Just then a puff of gold dust filled the room. As if in a trance, Sam opened the door to see his archenemy standing next to his beloved dog.

He's okay, Daring thought joyfully.

"DARING!" Sam roared.

Daring nearly smothered Sam with kisses and slobber until Mr. Harris stopped her. "What do you say to Basil, Sam?"

"I don't know what to say besides thank you," Sam said.

Basil smiled warmly at Sam. "Aw, it was nothing. I mean you should have seen me wrestle the guy to the ground."

"Really?" Sam said wide-eyed.

"No, I wish. I just saw your dog and knew that I had to get her back to you," Basil said, pausing to look at the dog, "Daring rescued herself once she had the chance."

"Eggnog coming up," Archie announced. Then, as if he had a second thought – a human thought, Archie asked,

"Y'ALL WANNA STAY FOR DINNAH?"

"That's a great idea, Archie." Mr. Harris turned to Mr. Pettibone. "Say you'll stay, please."

"Well, we left a Christmas tree in the parking lot."

Basil was quick to jump in. "We don't need a tree, Dad. I want to stay if it's okay with Sam."

"Are you kidding?" Sam said. "Sure it is!"

And so the press arrived, the television crew, the police, Lily, Fingers, the Crabs, the orchestra kids, and finally Dr. Fanny Sunshine Trout.

Archie kept cooking and serving while Daring kept having her photo taken.

Chief Butters announced that although the robber had escaped in all the chaos, he was sure he'd find him soon enough now that he had a really good description and especially since he was wearing handcuffs.

As cameras whirled, Daring stopped kissing Sam for just a moment, cocked her head, and then delivered the biggest, most wonderful, warmest and endearing bloodhound smile. *If only the Masons could see me now.*

Actually …

Mr. and Mrs. Mason always watched the evening news before going to bed. Christmas Eve in the Florida Keys was no exception.

"... And now from the picture-book pretty little town of Misty Harbor, Maine where a young boy is reunited with his dog, kidnapped a week ago..."

"I'll be darned if that doesn't look like Daring," Mrs. Mason said.

"Oh, you just miss that foolish little puppy," Mr. Mason reminded her.

"I suppose you're right, but still –"

"Let's say goodnight," Mr. Mason said, and they clicked off the television.

"Pucker up, Prudie girl," he flirted, as he had for the forty-odd years of their marriage. And with her lips in an impressive pucker, Prudie received her husband's good night smooch. A quick scratch behind each other's ears, followed by a mutual pat on the head and it was time to pull up the blanket and snuggle.

"You know, Doug," Prudie whispered, "I am pretty sure that was Daring.

"Shhhh, my love," Mr. Mason answered, as he burrowed his nose into the crook of her neck.

"Well, she looked like she found a good home," she said.

"Yes, I'm sure she did, Mr. Mason said, "You can stop worrying now."

Prudie Mason did just that. Finally, she could stop worrying about the little puppy with a mind of her own.

43
Christmas Morning

~

A text from Lily was waiting for Sam when he finally woke up on Christmas day. He had slept like a baby with Daring curled up next to him and not even the thought of opening his presents, or the luscious smell of Archie's breakfast bonanza had gotten him out of bed.

LC: It's a miracle
SH: I knO
LC: wz it rly Basil?
SH: yS
LC: It's NothA miracle
SH: I knO
LC: jst had 2 b pAtNt

Sam stretched out on his bed, his hand rested on Daring's head. The dog shifted position and put her head next to Sam's bare feet. Slowly at first, then more deliberately, Daring started licking Sam's toes. Then his ankles. Then the arch of Sam's foot.

"Stop that, Daring," Sam said, giggling, "It tickles."

Daring continued as Sam giggled harder and harder.

"Stop! It ...
TICKLES!!!"
"DAD!"

The following day Mr. Harris was on the phone with Dr. Trout.

"It's a miracle," Mr. Harris said. "The feeling is returning to his legs!"

"Yes, it's a miracle, all right," Dr. Hannah Sunshine Trout agreed, "A miracle named Daring Dog."

SKY BLUE PINK! Sam saw the colors of an Arctic sunset in his dream. He felt the wind on his face as he rode on a whale watch boat with his mother. She smiled at him and tousled his hair. "Over there, Sam!" she cried above the wind and he saw a majestic humpback whale rise out of the water and hurl its body in a full breach! He felt her touch, her fingers on his face, saw the corners of her eyes crinkle up when she smiled, heard her laugh and then heard her say... "I love you and Daddy very much, Sam. Tell Daddy that the eagle is intelligent and resourceful and rules the sky. It is able to transform itself into a human." A flutter of golden dust, a warm silky breeze ... and Sam turned over, re-arranged his pillows and drifted back to sleep.

The End

Acknowledgements

The Adventures of Daring Dog began as an idea for a movie. However, once I began to develop the characters, I knew that someday I had to write the book. As much fun as it is to see characters come alive on the screen, we sometimes lose the opportunity to tell the "back story" – the reason that people – and in this case, dogs – are compelled to do what they do.

My dear friend and colleague, Andrea Asimow, spent hours reading and re-reading the drafts of this book. Her editorial comments, peppered with a great sense of humor, helped me through the awesome task of turning a screen-play treatment into a book. Christine Cohen and Cathy Viner gave wonderful feedback and encouragement that convinced me that I was on the right track with my story. Terry Abrahamson took me to task and challenged me to a point where I revisited the story, took a closer look at my characters, then developed them until they became far more interesting to me, and hopefully to my readers. Peggy Bailey, a retired teacher of grades 3 and 4, poured over the final manuscript and made edits on nearly every page. In perfect teacher-penmanship, not only did Peggy make an edit, she cited her reasons. I will never be able to thank her enough. Lastly, Jane Gopan, a retired Boston schoolteacher, did the final proofreading of this manuscript. Many, many thanks to my sister. My granddaughters, Minna and Kaia loved the story from the moment I told it to them and I thank them for their confidence in me, as well as their love and support. Thomas Kerwin, who is the same age as the fictional Sam Harris, read the final manuscript carefully and gave me excellent feedback for which I am very appreciative. As they have throughout my career, my family and close friends have provided me with the love and comfort that make it possible for me to come back to reality when I let the creative juices take over.

My family and I have had many dogs in our lives. Most notably were Pedro, Clover and Worm, whose memory we keep close to our hearts. Clover was my first muse after he was able to squeeze his large body through a small car window and appear to have flown through it. After he passed away, we adopted a remarkable puppy from the Brewster, Massachusetts division of the Animal Rescue League of Boston. Penny was a Catahoula Leopard Dog mix who loved to run across the clam-flats near our Cape Cod home. In her younger years, Penny could run so fast that she appeared to be flying. Penny was often by my side as I read passages of my screenplay treatment aloud. I could usually tell if she approved.

Penny lived for thirteen and a half years. Her passing tore a hole in my heart and I promised myself never to get another dog, the heartbreak was too huge. Instead, I delighted in my grandchildren's dogs, Sam and Max, two irascible terriers, and my daughter's Yorkie/Maltese, Gogo, an army of one. It was enough for me until one evening when I opened my email and found a photo of a little dog thought to be a Brussels Griffon/mix (but later determined to be a Shih Tzu/Chihuahua) waiting to be rescued. I called my daughter and chastised her for sending it to me. "I'm through," I protested. Still, those soulful brown eyes drew me back. Two days later, Cathy Viner and I drove across Florida to adopt her. That was almost eight years ago, about three years after Penny had passed to Heaven, joined later by family dogs, beloved and sorely missed, Sam and Gogo.

Today, Stella Bella sits quietly in her bed next to my desk, content to snooze as I write. I reward her with a walk on the beach as often as I can, and as many loving hugs, kisses and snuggles as she will tolerate. Stella's friendship is a constant reminder that Life Is Good.

About the Author

~

Charlotte Jerace loves dogs, cats, birds, lions, tigers and whales. She has been anxious to introduce you to Daring Dog for a very long time. Before she began writing for children, Charlotte was a partner in a global benefits consulting firm where she received national recognition for her writing and creativity. Her notable awards include several Telly Awards, a New York Film Festival Award, and the Gold Quill from the International Association of Business Communicators. Her first short story, "Cannibals" was published by Provincetown Arts Magazine. A full-length novel, "Kentucky Rain", was published by CreateSpace in 2007. She was born on the rockbound coast of Maine, where she developed her appreciation for the ever-changing beauty of the ocean. It continues to be a source of inspiration, and the perfect place for her to count her blessings. An avid gardener and whale-watcher, Charlotte divides her time between Cape Cod and South Florida. When taking her daily beach walks, her dog, Stella, is always at her side.

Charlotte Jerace and her beloved rescue dog, Stella

Learn about Daring Dog's next adventure on the author's website
www.charlottejerace.com